TWO WOMEN IN ONE

TWO WOMEN IN ONE

Nawal el-Saadawi

*Translated by Osman Nusairi
and Jana Gough*

The Seal Press

First published in 1975 as *Imra'atan fi imra'a* by
Manshurat Dar al-Adab, Beirut.

This U.S. edition first published in 1986 by
The Seal Press.

Published by arrangement with Al Saqi Books,
26 Westbourne Grove, London, W2, England.
Copyright ©1985 by Al Saqi Books.

Manufactured in the United States of America.

Cover design by Deborah Brown.
Cover illustration is from *Coptic Textile Designs* by
M. Gerspach ©1975 by Dover Publications.

Library of Congress Cataloging-in-Publication Data:

Sa'dāwī, Nawāl.
Two women in one.

Translation of: *Imra'atan fi imra'ah.*
"U.S. edition"–T.p. verso.
I. Title.
PJ7862.A314413   1986   892'.736   86-3675

ISBN: 0-931188-40-7

The Seal Press
P.O. Box 13
Seattle, Washington 98111

To all young men and women; that they may realize, before it is too late, that the path of love is not strewn with roses, that when flowers first bloom in the sun they are assaulted by swarms of bees that suck their tender petals, and that if they do not fight back they will be destroyed. But if they resist, if they turn their tender petals into sharp protruding thorns, they can survive among hungry bees.

N.S.

It was the fourth of September. She stood with her right foot on the edge of the marble table and her left foot on the floor, a posture unbecoming for a woman — but then in society's eyes she was not yet a woman, since she was only eighteen. In those days, girls' dresses made it impossible for them to stand like that. Their skirts wound tightly round the thighs and narrowed at the knees, so that their legs remained bound together whether they were sitting, standing, or walking, producing an unnatural movement. Girls walked with a strange, mechanical gait, their feet shuffling along while legs and knees remained clamped, as if they were pressing their thighs together to protect something they were afraid might fall.

She had always been curious to know just what it was that might fall the minute a girl's legs were parted. Naturally inquisitive, she would constantly watch the worm-like movement of girls as they walked.

She did not look very different from these girls, except that she wore trousers, had long legs with straight bones and strong muscles, and could walk firmly, swinging her legs freely and striding out confidently. She was always surrounded by girls — she went to girls' schools with classes for girls only. Her

7

name always appeared among those of other girls. Bahiah Shaheen: the feminine ending of her name bound it like a link in a chain into lists of girls' names.

Since the human brain is incapable of perceiving the essence of things, everyone knew her as Bahiah Shaheen and no one ever penetrated her true essence.

People were always surprised by the way she walked, keeping a visible distance between her knees. She would pretend not to notice them staring at that gap. She would just keep walking, moving her legs, keeping them apart and putting each foot down with a firmness that she knew did not belong to Bahiah Shaheen.

On that day, her eighteenth birthday, she was standing in her usual way: right foot on the edge of the marble table, left foot on the floor. At the time, neither men nor women would assume such a posture. It required a pair of confident legs with flexible muscles and strong, sound bones. Childhood malnutrition had made most boys bow–legged. The most they would dream of doing was to lift one foot and balance it on the edge of a low wooden stand. She often saw boys standing this way. It was normal and permissible — but only for males.

The one man who could lift his foot higher and rest it on the edge of the table was Dr Alawi, the anatomy lecturer, who would sweep past the tables in his white coat and white glasses. When he stopped at a table, the male students would take their feet down from the stools and stand before him, their legs together. Dr Alawi, however, would lift his leg high and plant his foot confidently on the edge of the table, looking directly at the students with his unflinching blue gaze.

When he stood at her table, she would never take

her foot down. When he fixed his blue eyes on her, she would stare back at him with her own black eyes. She knew full well that black is stronger than blue, particularly where eyes are concerned. Black is the origin, the root that reaches back into the depths of the earth.

Holding the forceps in his white, blood–splattered fingers, he would stick his hand into the gaping stomach of a corpse, or grab at something in an arm, leg, head or neck, then bellow in his strident voice, 'What's this?' He would always pick the smallest of things — a tiny vein crossing the underside of a small muscle, a fine artery hidden under a fold of skin, or a nerve as delicate as a hair, so thin it could hardly be picked up by the forceps.

Eight girls stood around one corpse. More than one of them knew the names of all the veins, nerves and arteries by heart. No sooner did Dr Alawi ask what a particular object was than a sharp but low feminine voice rang out with the correct answer. He would always look at her, expecting her to answer, to prove to him that she knew, but she couldn't help it, she refused to be examined by anyone.

On that fourth of September, she felt that something big would happen to her She had the same feeling every fourth of September. When she opened her eyes in the morning the sun would be shining in an unusual way and her mother's eyes were glittering and sharp. 'On a day like this', she would whisper to herself, 'something big happened to my mother — she gave birth to me.' Each year she felt that something big would happen again on that day, something even bigger than being born. Whenever Bahiah whispered this idea to her mother, she would laugh that feminine laugh so typical of those times — holding back and letting go at the same time, producing a kind of staccato braying. 'Oh, come on, Bahiah', she would say.

Her mother never understood her. When Bahiah saw her mother in her usual place in bed, she would quietly creep in next to her and take her father's place. She would wind her small arms around her mother's huge neck just as she had seen him do. She somehow knew instinctively that her mother's body was the only thing that understood her.

In those days she loved to read fairy tales and myths. In one story there was a terrible god worshipped by the people of an enchanted city. This god could grasp any solid object and clench his fist, and when he opened his hand it would be gone. She was instinctively annoyed by this power, which threatened her very being. As a child she never understood this instinctive irritation, but in the end she came to understand it gradually. She then realized that she had actually understood it from the very beginning, from the moment she became aware that she had a body of her own, separate from her mother's.

This moment would always haunt her. The pain was like a knife tearing her flesh. None the less, it was not real pain. When her hand reached all the way around her own separate body, she jumped high in the air like a sparrow soaring with happiness, but she was no sparrow, and gravity pulled her back down. Since that fall she had recognized the weight of her own body. She knew it was heavier than she was and that the earth pulled it more strongly than she ever could, like her mother's arms pulling her again. With all the power she could muster, Bahiah had tried to make their two bodies one, but in vain. The eternal separation took place and the moment passed, never to return.

From childhood she had felt the tragedy of her own body, carrying it with her at every step and every cell. She burned with desire to return to where she had come from, to escape the field of gravity and free herself of that body whose own weight, surface and boundaries divided it from its surroundings: a consuming desire to dissolve like particles of air in the universe, to reach a final, total vanishing–point.

She used to stare at the picture of the magic god, carefully watching him crush things between his large fingers at a single touch. At night she would sometimes waken with a start, creep into her parents' bed and slip her small body between their naked bodies. Her father's big arms would push her roughly away, but her mother would look at her with eyes as black as her own and murmur affectionately, 'Go back to bed, Bahiah. You're a big girl now.'

The voice was affectionate. She felt its affection, like soft fingers caressing her body, turning in a circle, as if the fingers were defining her body, demarcating its boundaries with the outside world. Back in her own bed, this affection, which filled her with tenderness and reaffirmed her independent existence and separate private being, made her cry her heart out in silence, her body racked by sobs, the bed rocking under her. She would be swept by an uncontrollable desire for those fingers to abandon their false affection and to crush her, to free her from her own body for ever and to weld her mother and herself into one.

She closed her eyes and tried to sleep, but in vain. Fear gripped her, for a strange idea had crossed her mind: what if she wasted her whole life searching for or fleeing that moment? Terrified, she hid her head under the bedclothes. Her bedroom then filled with legendary ghosts and magic gods pressing down on her body to crush her, while she resisted with all her might, kicking and biting and crying out to her mother and father for help.

But it was not real fear that made her cry: it was a trick to deceive her mother, who had taught her deception by lying to her. She used to sleep in Bahiah's bed, promising not to leave her alone. But at midnight Bahiah would feel her creep out of bed and go to her father. Bahiah would then use a similar tactic. She knew that her quavering, pitiful cries would bring her mother back to her bed.

Her mother had never understood what Bahiah wanted. She used to stuff her with food. When she wasn't looking, Bahiah would spit the food out. She wondered how it was that her mother didn't understand her, since her mother had once been like her. Bahiah had asked her once, but she said that she could not remember. So Bahiah learnt that people deliberately forget real memories and replace them with imaginary ones.

Once, with a child's innocence, she told her mother that she had discovered she was a girl, not a boy — and undressed to prove it. But her mother slapped her hand, and told her 'Promise me never to do that again.' When Bahiah didn't answer, her mother slapped her face. But Bahiah still would not open her mouth to promise never to do it again. Instead her mind suddenly grasped a strange fact: pursing her lips and bowing her head, she realized that people suppress only real desires, because they are strong, while unreal desires are weak and need no laws to keep them in check. It was then that she began looking into all the taboos around her, trying to unravel people's real desires.

It was nothing less than the search for truth. When

Dr Alawi passed by the window of the dissecting room in his big car, seven pairs of female eyes would light up and fourteen irises swing towards him in unison. But Bahiah's deep black eyes remained focused on that strange sensation which reminded her that everything permissible is unreal. One of the students poked her sharply in the shoulder with a finger and said, 'Look.' She glanced out of the window to see a head, with slightly protruding eyes, emerging from the big car. The sharp finger dug her in the shoulder again: 'What do you think Bahiah?'

'He doesn't look real.'

Her fellow student patted her on the back with her soft hand and said sarcastically, 'Oh, you're hopeless.'

Seven mouths then opened with suppressed feminine laughter like gasps of eternally unquenchable deprivation. Their deprivation angered her more than their laughter. She flushed, collected her lancets and surgical tools, packed them into her leather satchel, and left the dissecting room. As she walked along in the open air, the smell of formalin and corpses leaving her nostrils, she realized that neither their deprivation nor their laughter angered her. She longed to confide in somebody about that strange sensation building up inside her, like a foetus growing day by day to reach its climax on the fourth of September every year, confirming to her that she was definitely not Bahiah Shaheen.

She left the college grounds and walked along Qasr al-Aini street, staring at passing faces as if searching for her real one. She stopped at the tram station, realizing that she was not searching for anything and that she was hungry and tired.

On the tram she sat with her back to one man, facing another. There was a man to her left and a man to her right. Rows and rows of men sat shoulder to shoulder in silence in front of her. Their lower bodies were immobile, fixed to their seats, while from the waist up they shook slowly and rhythmically with the motion of the tram. When it stopped their heads jerked violently back and their eyes popped open in fright. Once reassured that their heads were still in the right place, they closed their eyes and slept.

They were government employees. Their bodies were all the same shape, their features and suits, fingers and shoes identical, as if the government had stamped them from a mould, minted them like coins in the same conical shape. They sat side by side, and despite the thick padding of their suits, their shoulders somehow drooped, as if they bore some eternal burden — invisible, but present nevertheless. They moved as if shifting that burden from shoulder to shoulder. They seemed to sleep, but the flickering movement of eyes under lids betrayed the fact that their sleep was not real. When they opened their eyes and looked at her, she realized that their waking was unreal too. Then everything in them and around them became unreal. If their lips parted to reveal their teeth, you could not tell whether they were smiling or grimacing. When their fingers moved as they got on or off the tram, they might be exchanging greetings or threats. Everything about them became confused. Their every aspect was identical to its opposite. A smile was a threat, truth a lie, virtue vice, and love hate. Mannerisms, gestures and meanings were alike to the point of suffocation.

She craned her neck out the tram window and took a deep breath. When she recovered, she realized how much governments deform people. An adult might be reduced to child size, but the bones of his skull would

14

betray his real age. His suit and tie might suggest that he is of the ruling classes, but his walk reveals that he is one of the ruled.

She saw them everywhere, filling the streets and stuffed into trams. They went in and out of doors, lobbies, and buildings with their small bodies and their wide, padded shoulders, with their large skulls, hunched backs and wide parted lips, grinning as if grimacing, or grimacing as if grinning. Human beings transformed by some potent power, by some terrible non-human force that had turned them into other, inhuman beings.

She got off the tram and walked home. In the distance she saw a man who looked just like other men. Wide shoulders, big skull, bowed back. She averted her gaze and quickened her step, anxious to get home. But the man called her name and when she turned she saw the face of her father. He must have seen terror in her face, for his eyes widened in surprise and he asked, 'What's the matter, Bahiah?'

She hid her face in her hands and rushed home.

Although Bahiah was still pale, her mother did not notice when she let her in. Bahiah was always pale. It was difficult for someone like her mother to distinguish between degrees of paleness. That called for an ability to observe closely over long periods. But her mother could not bring herself to look Bahiah in the face. Her eyes could never meet her daughter's gaze. Bahiah saw this as proof that her mother had deceived her since childhood, just as her father had done. He would turn up at home, with his tall, bulky frame, his straight back, and those big strong hands that could slap her down; but really he was only a government employee among thousands of others.

There were eighteen lighted candles on the white table. Her mother stuffed Bahiah with sweets, and Bahiah spat them out when her mother turned around; her father smiled at her, but she was suspicious of his smile. Everything about her father had become dubious. Doubt is like a candle — it has a red flame and burns needle-sharp: she still remembered how her finger stung. It was the same table, but there was just one candle. She was just one year old.

The bright red flame had seemed like part of herself. Her small, soft body crawled on the floor, sticking so close that she seemed part of it. She had been separated from the universe, though her hand could not yet trace a full circle round her body. Her hand was small, her body big, vast, seeming to fill the tall space between ceiling and floor. When she stretched out her hand to explore her legs, she could not tell whether they belonged to her or to the chair. Did the red flame come from the candle or from herself? Goaded by doubt, she decided to find out: she stretched out her finger and was burned by the flame. Now she knew the difference between the flame and her own eyes. Doubt and pain shaped the outline of her body and every part of her began to acquire its own special form.

From across the white table, over the eighteen candles, she heard her mother's voice: 'Happy birthday, Bahiah.' Sudden astonishment. She could not believe she was eighteen. Had the earth really revolved eighteen times around the sun? She had no idea how she came to ask such a question, but an invisible silken thread seemed to link her own cycle to the world's. When she gazed at the disc of the moon, those silken, wire-like threads stretched between them and pulled them together. But the earth's gravity was stronger. Torn between earth and moon, she seemed calm on the surface, but deep inside her was a whirlpool, resisting the pull from all sides. Something small and round, like an inflated balloon, burst within her, and a tiny egg, pin-head sized, came out, its one staring eye seeking the eternal moment of contact in order to vanish into the world for ever.

Her face glowed red in the light of the candles. Her father thought she was blushing, as befits a girl of only eighteen. But she was not eighteen, nor was she a girl. 'What does it mean to be a girl?' she asked her parents and her fellow students in the dissecting room. When Dr Alawi heard the question, he dipped his metal forceps into the open stomach of the dead woman whose body lay before him and took out her womb: a small, pear-sized triangle of flesh soft on the surface and wrinkled within. The base of the triangle was at the top and the two sides converged downward.

His blue gaze fixed her black eyes. He smiled, but she did not smile back. Drawing her to the next table, he said in his professorial tone, 'As for man, here he is.' With the tips of his forceps, he held up the penis. She saw a wrinkled piece of black skin like old excrement.

When she got home she sat in front of her mother and told her to look at her carefully and then asked, 'Am I Bahiah?' Her mother gave an eternally suppressed feminine gasp and said, 'Oh come on, girl!' Her mother had never understood her. But she understood her mother. If she stared at her long enough she could see her coiled womb crouching at the base of her stomach. She could see its muscles clenching and un-clenching in a quick continuous pulse, like the pulse of the world in the night silence, its motion invisible and imperceptible, like the motion of the earth. She wanted with all her might to squeeze this womb, to halt its secret mad movement, to still it for ever. But her mother lowered her eyes, for she could never look directly at her for long. Somewhere deep in her core she was hiding something, burying it in the folds of her very self and binding it with layer upon layer of her insides, turning it invisible, keeping its motion ever hidden and eternally secret.

'Eternity' was a word she had never understood. One day after another, the blood flowing in her veins following the cycle of the moon, the cell swelling within her and bursting at the very same instant. The tiny egg spun madly like the earth on its axis. With one eye, she would gaze at the universe seeking to annihilate herself, but in vain, the same vain frustration every time, with each futile cycle of the moon. Anger mounted within her like warm blood. It gathered, rose, and rotated in a cycle of its own within the domain of her body. She felt it unmistakably in her cells, an insistent, nagging feeling, telling her that one day, one given, fateful day, something momentous would happen to her.

She had never used a diary. Nor did she look at the calendar hanging in her father's room, the one she always saw him consulting as he peeled off the passing days. Every morning he would tear off a day in the same way and with the same motion, scrunching it into a ball between his fingers, but she would pull it out of his hand, shouting, 'Stop! Leave it alone!' This time, before he had raised his large hand from the sheet of paper, she thought she had made a mistake, that the sun was not shining any brighter than usual, that her mother's eyes were as always, and that the strange feeling that had come over her was just another of her many assorted illusions. She waited for her father to tear off the sheet of paper as usual, but this time he stopped. Instead she heard his voice behind her saying, 'Happy birthday, Bahiah.' She turned, saw the figure 4 on the white sheet of paper, and the blood drained from her face.

She looked around her as she walked down the street. When she heard a voice behind her, she stopped and turned as though someone had called her name. Suddenly she realized that the voice was calling a different name, one that happened to rhyme with hers, something like Kufiah, Najiah, Aliah or Zakiah.

On the tram she felt someone riding behind her, following her. When she got out at Qasr al-Aini street she imagined she heard his steps. As she went in through the college gate, so did he.

But she lost him in the spacious, crowded grounds. Voices and features intermingled and she felt as if she were sinking in the sea alone, with no one to see or recognize her; her face had become just like her fellow students', so that there was no difference between Bahiah, Aliah, Suad and Yvonne.

At that moment she grasped the meaning of death. She had been searching for death in the corpses laid out in the dissecting room. But death is like life; it dwells not in corpses but only in a living brain, a brain fully alive and able to detect the slightest nuance, the most deeply hidden and intimate sensation: like the feeling of loss experienced by a particle of air floating in the universe and resisting being lost among millions of other particles; or the suppressed desire of a drop of water resisting dissolution in the sea, that desperate, insane resistance at the peak of frustration which breeds complete submission like eternal silence. Anyone looking at her face at that moment would have thought her blind and dumb; her body seemed still, even though her feet moved mechanically over the ground. Everything had the same colour and shape to her. All bodies were similar, and all gestures and voices. She found herself running aimlessly, fleeing the college grounds, fleeing the deadly sameness within and without, inside her body and in the outside world.

She had her own favourite, secluded corner, opposite the college fence, behind the huge building. She would sit there on a wooden stool, leaning forwards, gazing at a patch of earth the size of the palm of her hand, where no green grass had ever grown. Unlike the rest of the earth around it, this furrowed patch was always mud-coloured, and between ridges, millions of tiny, ant-sized creatures were always coming and going.

'Bahiah'.

The name sounded as if it belonged to someone else. She leapt up from her stool. As she did, she realized that she had a body of her own, one she could move and shake without other bodies moving and shaking. She also had a name of her own, and when that name was called she would look up in surprise. She might even ask, 'Who's that?' She got a shock every time she heard her name and a hidden feeling would tell her that someone was calling her own name, selecting her from among millions of other bodies, singling her out among the billions of other creatures floating in the universe.

The blood drained from her face. She became deathly pale, like a ghostly stone statue or the faces of the corpses lined up one after the other on marble tables in the dissecting room. She looked at the colour of her face in the mirror in the women's room, and when her fingers touched her forehead, they were ice-cold. She knew she was trembling, and she wanted to escape the voice that called her, that summons issued directly and specifically to her, that miraculous power that was able to pick her out among all the others. She wanted to escape. With unaccustomed speed, she ran and hid among the crowd of girl students, her body disappearing among theirs. When their heads moved, so did hers — right, left, backwards and forwards. They protected her like a shield. There she stayed, hidden among them, unable to venture out. For outside was a supernatural force, capable of picking her out of crowds, and of distinguishing her body from others. A dreadfully potent force. The moment her head showed, this force would pull her with a magnetic power stronger than gravity. Once it had drawn her into its electromagnetic field, she would spin madly and helplessly in its orbit until the revolutions destroyed her.

She sensed that danger growing ever greater within her, a danger that threatened inevitably to destroy her. She felt as if a germ lived inside her, eating her body away cautiously and quietly, gradually destroying it; or that her body would suddenly be crushed under the wheels of a bus, or on the tramlines, and no one would come to her rescue. When she heard a cry and leaned her head out the tram window to see a body torn to shreds on the rails, she felt that the body was hers, the pale face hers, the red blood spattered over the tar her own. But the tram moved on again and she found her body where it had always been, intact on the seat. Her blood still flowed through her veins: it had not gushed out. A hidden certainty told her that the day had not yet come, that she was still Bahiah Shaheen, hard-working, well-behaved medical student, daughter of Muhammad Shaheen, superintendent of the Ministry of Health.

She entered the college just as she did every day, headed for the lecture hall and took her usual seat, the last in the back row on the left. Anyone would have thought she was fast asleep, but in fact she was wide awake, seeing the male students more clearly than ever before. She watched them push through the door, treading on each other's feet, their bags under their arms bulging with anatomy books. Left hands clutching their precarious spectacles and right hands stretched out to push other bodies out of the way. They raced for the front seats in the lecture hall. Panting and out of breath, they grabbed their seats and opened their notebooks with fingers red and swollen from the fight to clamber on to the tram. Giving their fingers a quick rub, they thrust them into their pockets. A student might bury his head in his notebook to revise previous lectures, or crane his neck left or right to whisper a joke (usually obscene) to a classmate. When the lecturer arrived, a hushed silence fell over the hall. Each student could hear the rumbling of his neighbour's empty stomach. The lecturer stepped slowly and quietly to the podium. His voice was quiet and his body too, his limbs relaxed and his cells secure, basking in the kind of reassurance felt by the stomach after a good meal, or the buttocks after relaxing in a comfortable chair. The students closed their eyes and dreamed of this relaxation, this self-assurance. They realized it was the fruit of a childhood dream, born when they first saw the gleam in their fathers' eyes at the mere mention of the word 'doctor'.

She would sit in the back row, not seeing their eyes, only their backs, as they pored over their notebooks. She imagined them permanently hunched and doubled over and was almost surprised to see them move about at the end of the lecture. They would jump up and rush for the door, tripping over each other and elbowing each other out of the way. When an elbow edged sneakily into a girl student's breast, her lips would part almost imperceptibly. With an inaudible suppressed whisper the girl would say 'Ah . . . ' and place her bulging satchel protectively over her chest. The touch of the soft breast would pass like a serum from elbow to shoulder to neck. Muscles contracted, features froze and eyes became taut as a rope stretched to its breaking-point: seemingly static, while its inner cells tremble invisibly in a mad, violent movement against the pull. The eye muscles twisted towards anything that had the softness of flesh, whether breast, bottom, or leather satchel. Each male student would unconsciously take a bite of his satchel and chew it. When he realized that it was only leather he would flush and try to hide the holes all over his bag with the palms of his hand. In the tram he could not stand it any more. He would find himself inadvertently pressed against some woman's breast. At midnight he would close his anatomy books and go to bed, but the body would refuse to sleep, for the stimulant would have congealed like the tip of a boil needing only the slightest touch to burst.

She didn't like the male students. She didn't like the way they rushed through the door with their thick glasses, straining eyes and angled elbows. She did not like the way they grabbed the front seats, showing her their bowed backs and exposing, above their white collars, their porous brown skin with its stubble and with the tiny imperfections scattered like sores.

She would look and then whisper something to a girl student, who would gasp with that suppressed feminine laugh and say, 'Oh, come on, Bahiah, start thinking about your future.'

Some hidden insistent feeling told her that her future did not lie in those long, boring lectures, nor in getting a medical degree and hanging a shingle in the square saying 'Dr Bahiah Shaheen', nor in settling her ass in a comfortable seat behind the wheel of a car. Something told her that all this was meaningless, like a blank sheet of paper or a dark night without a single star, as if the whole world had become black or white, it really didn't matter which, so long as it was all one colour.

It was then that she realized the absurdity of the world around her, of life, of the lecturer posing with a cigarette drooping from the corner of his mouth, of the bowed backs and those spotted necks.

She put her books and notebooks in her satchel, edged out of her seat and left through the back door of the lecture hall. She was on her own in the spacious college grounds. Moving her legs freely in her usual gait, she asked herself what she wanted to do with her life. She left the question unanswered; it hung in the air before her swinging slightly like a pendulum. She stamped the ground hard with one foot and realized that she wanted to do something concrete with her life, something definite. She could do it with a pen-point on a blank sheet of paper; she could touch it with her fingertip just as certainly as she could touch her body, feeling its external boundaries under her clothes, just as she could distinguish it from all the other bodies and lift it from the ground by moving her feet.

In her small bedroom, she gazed up at the ceiling. She saw herself sitting on her small red chair at her red desk, on which lay her notebooks and her textbook with its blue cover and white label. Name: Bahiah Shaheen. Subject: 1st Year Anatomy. She tore a clean sheet of paper from her exercise book. With a movement of her small hand, she drew a clear line with the nib of her pen, a line whose shape she recognized as her own. She knew too that the hand was hers, and the fingers around the pen. She could will them to make her distinct lines on the blank page, drawing a full circle and two smaller circles inside it — making a face and a pair of eyes glaring up from the white paper, a pair of wide black eyes like her own, staring at her woman to woman. She looked at her lines on the sheet of paper as carefully as she would look at her own features. She knew them as she knew her own face, never confusing it with other faces. She could distinguish her face and touch the lines on the paper with her finger, with the same certainty with which she would touch her own body and feel its external boundaries under her clothes.

Her father opened the door and she slipped the piece of paper under the textbook. But his large fingers picked up the book and extracted the drawing. He slapped her small hand with his broad palm and said, 'What do you mean by wasting your time scribbling?' He crumpled the sheet of paper and tossed it into the dustbin.

When he left she glanced at her familiar, crumpled drawing lying in the rubbish. She stared at it for a long time, just as she gazed at her face in the mirror. Then she pulled out a fresh sheet of paper and with determination she drew her lines, her invisible electric wires of fine silken threads, the colour of air, linking her with the drawing on the white sheet of paper, affirming her ability to distinguish the movement of her hand, the shape of her fingers, the length of her nose and the black of her eyes.

When she heard her father's voice as he sat in the salon slumped in his Asyut-style chair, she hid the piece of paper under the textbook and began to read aloud, in a voice that rang in her ears like somebody else's. The name on the cover seemed strange to her, as if it was the name of some other pupil, docile and obedient, doing what she was told, getting on with her homework and concealing her real self in the folds of the hidden sheet of paper.

Ever since she first became aware of life, she had wondered why all the things she loved were taboo. Even food — the stuff they made her eat was the kind she hated most. Her mother shovelled it into her mouth and as soon as her back was turned, Bahiah spat it out. Her father hated her drawings. Let him see her take a sheet of paper and he would tear it to shreds or crumple it up and throw it out with the household rubbish.

Her father stood like a vast, high barrier between her and her real self, blocking her way, guarding the entrance to the house with the bulk of his body, his loud coarse voice, huge palms and wide eyes. When his voice rang out, calling her name, she felt he was calling somebody else but she would answer anyway: 'Yes, father.' 'Have you done your homework?' he would ask, and she would reply politely and obediently, 'Yes, father.' When she heard the word 'yes' she realized that the voice was definitely not her own.

Only when her father had vanished from the salon and she felt alone in her room could she hear her real voice. She could distinguish its features and tone just as she could define the features of her own body. Her thin fingers removed the white label bearing the false name on the blue cover. As the nib of her pen moved over the white page, she defined things as she really saw them. When she drew her father, she gave him two red eyes and a black handlebar moustache, huge hands and fingers coiled round a long stick.

Her father did not have a black handlebar moustache. But on her way to and from school every day, she would see the policeman in his street-corner wooden shelter. All she saw of his face was a black handlebar moustache. She always quickened her step when she passed him, and sometimes ran home without stopping. The long stick was the one that was shaken at her every morning as she sat at her wooden desk in the classroom, the teacher's voice ringing out as sharply as her father's: 'Bahiah Shaheen. Have you done your homework?' At first she thought the teacher was calling somebody else and she pursed her lips in silence, but the sharp voice would ring out once more: 'Bahiah Shaheen!' Then she would jump up and reply with that polite, obedient 'Yes, Miss.' Friday was the only day she really liked, since school was closed. She would slip out of her narrow bed and onto her red chair, tear a sheet of paper from the middle of her exercise book, take her pen in her small fingers and move her hand over the page, drawing her lines. Sometimes she would take from her bag a red, blue or green pencil that she had bought with her pocket money from the shop near the school or borrowed from a classmate. Then she would colour in the drawing. She gave the tree green leaves and the sea blue water; blood she made red. How did she know that the colour of blood was red?

The first spot of red blood she had ever seen was on her small, white knickers. She would draw that spot like a deep red circle in the middle of the blank sheet of paper. The young girl's eyes were large and frightened. Her body was small and thin like a sparrow's trembling behind a wall. There were also many staring eyes, like full circles. With her small swollen fingers, she buried her knickers in a hole behind the wall. She walked out in the street without knickers. The cold wind passed between her legs, billowing her dress, but she pulled it down firmly with both hands, defying the wind. She walked along the tarmac street, her bag bulging with books.

As she neared the wooden shelter, a deep red drop of blood trickled down between her legs and onto the asphalt. It lay on the ground in a red circle that widened to grow as big as the sun. The policeman with his handlebar moustache stared at her. He poked his nose out of the shelter, sniffing the blood. She threw her bag to the ground and ran home breathlessly.

She moved her head across the pillow heavily and saw the leather bag, bulging with anatomy books, on top of her desk. Above the desk were notebooks, a skull and a mug of water with a red rose in it. Glancing out of the corner of her eye at the calendar hanging on the wall, she remembered that she had an examination. She spread out her lecture notes and books and sat gazing at the skull. It was the skull of someone who had died some years ago. She had bought it from the dissecting room attendant for three and a half Egyptian pounds. The year before it would have cost just one pound, but prices had gone up and corpses were scarce and now fetched black-market rates. The undertaker, dissecting room attendant and cemetery guard had formed a partnership. When some un-known person with no next of kin was run over by a tram and killed, the undertaker would immediately appear, followed by a 'father' hired by the hour. The 'father' would throw himself on the dead body and weep crocodile tears. He would then sign for the body, which was released to him as his personal property to do with as he wished, just as a father owns a son and can do as he likes with him.

The hired father would then sell the corpse to the

cemetery guard, who would sell it to the undertaker, who would sell it either to the dean of the medical school or to some rich student who wanted to study it at home without bothering to show up at the dissecting room every day. Bahiah looked closely at the skull. She saw the long crevices between the bones, resembling deep wounds, the prominent cheek-bones, the deep eye-sockets and the tapering jaws above the deep gaps between the teeth.

It was like the face of the child in tattered clothes who climbed onto the tram one day. He carried boxes of pins, matchboxes and a few combs. He called out his wares hoarsely, hopping from one tram to another on his one leg. He looked at people with his deep sunken eyes, searching among the faces for one with the features of a mother or father, who would reach into his pocket for a piastre or two and buy a comb or a box of pins.

But the faces on the tram were not those of fathers and mothers; instead they were those stunningly similar faces stamped out by the government like coins, sitting shoulder to shoulder in silence, their lower bodies immobile and fixed to their seats, their upper parts shaking slowly and rhythmically with the motion of the tram. Their huge skulls swung back and forth like pendulums. Their broad, padded shoulders were stuck to each other, their ties wound round their necks like hangmen's ropes. When the tram stopped, their heads jerked back violently. They leapt from their seats, holding their heads and staring around them, their yellow eyes wide and fearful. Suddenly a child's scream filled the air.

Round yellow eyes turned to the body, mangled under the wheels of the tram. Pins, matchboxes and combs lay scattered on the ground. The red spot shone on the asphalt, and the red circle widened like the sun, while the hollow eyes gazed out under the iron wheels like two deep holes in the belly of the earth.

They all ran their hands anxiously over their heads, necks, arms and thighs. Reassured that their heads were still on their shoulders, their bodies on the seats and their blood still coursing through their veins, they parted their lips and let out long, deep sighs. And their eyes gleamed with concealed delight. Some of them shook hands, congratulating each other on their escape and praising God for His great mercy, for the torn body under the wheels was not theirs but some-one else's. They raised their hands to heaven and murmured a prayer of thanksgiving, under the illu-sion that they were bribing Allah with those recita-tions (for He might destroy them at any moment), so that their necks would remain on their shoulders for ever and ever.

Bahiah turned the skull so that its hollow eyes faced the wall. She closed her anatomy book, reached behind the bed, pulled out the white painting and stood it against the wall. She sat on a small mattress on the floor, her brushes and paints beside her.

Her room was in total darkness except for a spot of white light shining on the painting from a small lamp. It was dead of night, her father was sound asleep. No voices and no movement except the rustle of the brush, criss-crossing the smooth surface. With a light motion of her fingers she willed her hand in whatever direction she wanted. She opened her eyes as wide as she could, warding off sleep. She gazed at her lines and at the coloured spot for hours.

Sometimes her hand would slap all those similar faces with purposeful brush strokes. She tore away the stretched mask of flesh with her fingers, dragging the torn body out from under the wheels and filling the slender skull with flesh. The two sunken holes became a pair of black eyes like her own.

In the morning she woke to the sound of her father's voice, shrill as an alarm clock. She put on her black trousers and white blouse, picked up her bulging leather satchel and walked towards the tram, striding along confidently, moving her legs freely. When she saw the sameness of the faces on the tram, she pursed her lips angrily. When she saw the other female students, walking with that strange mechanical gait, their legs held tightly together, she realized that they belonged to one species and she to another. She stood in the dissecting room, one foot propped on the marble table, the other leg, long and straight, of sound bone and muscle, planted on the floor. From the corner of her eye she saw the legs of the male students, their swollen red noses and their backs hunched over the corpses. She looked around astonished, as if she had lost her way. But there was the lancet between her fingers. The blue anatomy book bore the familiar white label: 'Name: Bahiah Shaheen. Subject: 1st Year Anatomy', which never failed to astonish her.

As she worked her way down through the block of flesh immersed in formalin, her lancet hit a hard object, which she managed to extract. It fell onto the marble table, sounding like a piece of gravel. The lancet cut it in half, and it turned out to be a dark clot of congealed blood. One of the female students said, with that suppressed feminine laugh, 'Goodness, I thought it was a bullet!' Another girl craned her neck to see, staring at the open heart in amazement: 'A bullet in the heart!' A third gasped and clapped her hand over her mouth: 'How sad!' A fourth sighed audibly: 'If only it was me.'

None of the familiar ideas about death could be found in the dissecting room. Here death was unreal. The corpse was not a dead man. The blood clot, congealed like a bullet in the heart, might stir a suppressed desire buried deep in the soul, like a heart rent apart, like blood arrested in its absurd cycle and congealing in the veins. It was death, both feared and desired; sought after, evaded and imagined everywhere, anywhere, in the mortuary.

Bahiah turned to the girl who had said, 'If only it was me' and asked, 'Do you want to die?' The girl gasped in astonishment and disapproval: 'Death? God forbid!' Bahiah now understood the tragedy. She knew why human beings hide their real desires: because they are strong enough to be destructive; and since people do not want to be destroyed, they opt for a passive life with no real desires.

Bahiah grasped this end of the thread and set out to seize the other, then realized that there was no other end, only the bottomless abyss itself. She gathered up her lancets and dissection instruments, put them in her leather satchel and left the room. She strode out into the college grounds with her long quick steps. With each stride her feeling of imminent danger mounted. She wished she could go back to the dissecting room, but a hidden feeling drew her towards that very danger, to the brink of the bottomless abyss.

'Bahiah'. The name rang in her ear and she jumped. As she did, she realized that she had a body of her own which she could move and stir without the world moving with it, and that she had a name of her own the sound of which would make her jump. Every time she heard her name called, she was astonished. What an extraordinary power, which could distinguish her name from all other names! What a miraculous power that picked out her body from among the millions of other floating bodies!

When she stopped, she discovered that she was still in the college grounds, standing in front of a large painting hanging on a small dark green door. She stopped no longer than thirty seconds, and was about to head back towards the dissecting room to continue her work, to remain at it for ever. But thirty seconds can change the course of a life; in thirty seconds a bomb can explode, transforming the face of the city and the earth. Life's crucial events happen all of a sudden, sometimes in the twinkling of an eye. Insignificant things occur slowly, taking their time, sometimes even dragging on for a lifetime.

When she looked up from the painting she realized that someone was standing in front of her. Not just anyone. He was the sort of person you have to look at, even if only for a few seconds. But that brief moment is enough to freeze those features before your eyes for ever. When the first moment had passed, she managed to stifle her surprise and return the stare. With her natural inquisitiveness, she scrutinized the unusual features, trying to understand what made them so extraordinary. The forehead was commonplace, the eyes ordinary; she wondered how such ordinary features could make up such a strange, extraordinary face.

He was directly in front of her, his right foot on the threshold of the door to the exhibition. He would have bumped into her had he not happened to look up and see her. Then their eyes met and she realized that the secret behind this extraordinary face lay in the way his eyes moved. It was strange, different from the other male students. Their eyes seemed not to see or do anything. They just opened like mirrors in which things were reflected. The eyes of the male students did not really see, or rather, they did not see things as they really were.

When his eyes moved in front of hers, she felt as if he were seeing her. It was the first time she had ever been seen by any eyes other than her own. Only in a mirror had she been aware of being seen by a pair of black eyes — her own. In the street, on the tram or at college, she realized that eyes were incapable of seeing her or distinguishing her from thousands of others, that she was lost among the sameness of bodies and that nothing could save her from being lost, except her own hand when it touched her body, reminding her that she had a body of her own; or when it took to drawing on the white canvas, making its motion visible, with clear lines distinct from the outside universe by their own external boundaries and their own roundness, thanks to a strong deliberate motion, with which she would destroy other wills, destroy the body, unmask the features, tear away the white label on the blue cover bearing the false name.

She saw his unusual eyes examining her face as she herself examined it in the mirror, piercing her eyes through long, narrow corridors leading to her very depths. One more moment was all he needed to reach the end. But she jerked her head away. She was afraid of reaching ends. She feared arrival, the impossibility of returning to where she had been; she was afraid that by a magic touch she would become somebody other than Bahiah Shaheen, somebody who was her real self.

She had never known exactly who that real self was. But she had always been sure that she was not Bahiah Shaheen, hard-working, well-behaved medical student, the girl with the light brown skin standing hesitantly before the door.

The word 'hesitant' does not apply here, however. For in fact she did not hesitate for a moment. She was drawn by a mysterious desire to press ahead and not to stop until she had reached the dangerous end. She was aware that she was heading there inevitably: it was her destiny. She was going there in no ordinary manner; rather, she was drawn by the strength of her desire to know her own destiny and by the intensity of her fear of that knowledge, a fear so great that it helped to drive her there.

If she were really Bahiah Shaheen, she would have turned, taken a step backwards and gone into the dissecting room. Today would have been like yesterday, and like tomorrow. She would have fallen back into the whirlpool of everyday life and everyday faces. But she was not Bahiah Shaheen, she was another diabolical being, born of neither her mother nor her father. Her features resembled those she saw in the mirror, but they were more intense. Her eyes were darker, the tilt of her nose more pronounced. Her complexion was not pale, but brown — burning and red, the colour of blood.

She did not like Bahiah Shaheen. She could see her defects all too clearly. She hated that polite obedient voice. She was irritated by that placid look which did not see things, but allowed them to be reflected from her, like a watery surface. She hated that nose which was not sufficiently upturned. She despised that paleness, whose real cause she knew. It was the paleness of a complexion drained of blood by fear, a fear that people seek to hide.

Bahiah Shaheen was afraid of her real self, of that other self dwelling within her, that devil who moved and saw things with the sharpest powers of perception. Her nose had a strange sharp tilt, like the edge of a sword. With that blade she cut the world in two and pressed ahead mercilessly and without hesitation, to meet the end, the end of the end, even if that meant the bottomless abyss itself.

But Bahiah Shaheen was hesitant. She would stop half-way, for she was afraid of ends. The end, she felt, was final, it was the high frightening summit, the point suspended in space with nothing before or behind it, the destructive summit, after which there is only extinction. She stood in the middle of the road. She knew she would stop there, but felt safe at that middle resting-point, in the centre of the tightrope, where the two split forces were equal. She was weightless, her resistance nil. It was the point of total stillness and complete unthreatened security. In other words, it was the point of death.

Bahiah Shaheen did not know that she stood on the brink of death itself and could not escape it. Her mind could not grasp that truth. In her funny naive way, she believed that she would somehow find safety by avoiding danger, by steering clear of any dangerous situations. Her mind could not see that she already stood at the heart of danger itself, and that any movement was a step towards safety, towards life. But she did not know how to save herself, or even why she had to do it. In other words, she did not know the purpose of her life.

When she moved her head to one side, he smiled that strange smile. At that moment she did not see it. He whispered softly, 'Bahiah Shaheen?'

The question surprised her and she stammered. But she quickly realized what was wrong, saw the name on the white name tag and answered hesitantly, 'Yes.'

He put out his hand: 'I'm Saleem Ibrahim.'

It was the first hand ever to envelop hers. His palm was the same size as her own, so were his long thin fingers. A real flesh-and-blood hand whose warmth spread through her palm, asserting its reality, for it was the same temperature as her own. The blood coursing through the veins of his hand beat with the pulse in her own wrist, like the earth beneath her and the air around her. He gazed into her wide black eyes, now full of that panic which surfaces only when danger is sensed. Panic widened his eyes too, but he checked himself and brought his gaze under control. In thirty seconds they knew each other in a way that would have taken another man and woman fifty years.

'I congratulate you on the exhibition.'

Overcome by sudden shyness, she blushed and stammered, 'I'm still just starting out.'

There were only three or four students at the exhibition. There were thousands of them at the medical school, but why should medical students be interested in an art exhibition? What good was a painting, a story or a piece of music to them? The dissecting room and the lectures, learnt by rote, parrotted back in examinations, and then forgotten for ever — nothing else mattered.

They stood before the painting, shoulder to shoulder. He was the same height as her. They stood side by side. His leg was just like hers. Only a small distance separated them, just room enough for a little air to pass between their bodies. A distance as long as she was tall, but hair-thin. It was an insulating distance, made of air, a substance other than that of their bodies. And it was very fine, like the blade of a sword separating one body from another and cutting through the flesh.

39

She was struck by a sense of amazement as in a dream, when momentous events happen in seconds; when you meet a stranger and know him, when you meet the dead and shake hands with them, when you can fly, arms, legs and all, or sink to the bottom of the sea without drowning, or walk a tightrope without falling, or see a house destroyed and rebuilt in seconds, and suddenly everything becomes possible in the twinkling of an eye.

She was used to that sense of amazement in her dreams. But now she was wide awake. She tried to make sure she was really awake, but failed. The only way was to touch her own body. But she had done that in dreams too, when she was not sure if she was asleep or not. This failure frightened her, for she could never be sure of anything in her life. Any attempt to make sure only increased her doubts.

His black eyes were fixed on the painting, which was black as night; the white dots looked like stars, but they were not stars, more like tiny diamonds. No, not really diamonds either, but small eyes, glittering with transparent tears. No, not eyes but a pair of small eyes in the face of the thin pale child walking alone in the street, tiny fingers red and swollen from the sharp end of the ruler: twenty strokes on each hand for losing the bag. At the bend in the street the big man with the handlebar moustache grabbed the child by the arm. The bag fell to the ground. With puny arms and legs, the child struck at the big legs, but they were strong and gaped like destiny's jaws. The child lay between those legs, face down on the asphalt near the wall. A fine trickle of blood streamed from her nostrils down her face; it would clot before her father saw it. But her father had looked into her eyes and known from the paleness that she was still bleeding. He searched between her arms and legs for the wound. When he saw the red circle as clear as the sun, he raised his big palm and slapped the child's face.

She glanced at the quick gleam in his eyes, and at a tiny muscle that twitched under his left eye. She gestured to the other painting, but he asked her in a low voice, 'Did you cry when you were a baby?'

She stuttered in amazement. Thinking back to her childhood dreams — the mythical god, her father, the policeman, the school and the sharp end of the ruler rapping her small fingers — she answered, 'They used to hit me on account of someone else called Bahiah Shaheen, who was obedient and well-behaved.'

He gave a short laugh and looked at the other painting — medical students with their thick spectacles and angular elbows crowding round a lecturer pulling a cart, crying his wares like a salesman, selling copies of his lectures, which he had printed on a hand duplicator. At the college gate were women in black gallabiahs and headcloths they had tied round their necks. They were following a corpse out of the dissecting room. At the tram station, a blind man was being led by a lame woman. Behind them were children with bare bottoms. Large heads, alike as coins struck from the same mould, looked on from inside the tramcars. On the corner lurked the policeman with the black moustache.

Standing close to her and motionless, he whispered, 'Bahiah'.

She shuddered at the sound of his voice. The name Bahiah had become very special. It was not like the name Bahiah — any Bahiah — but referred to her in particular, her and nobody else, her to the exclusion of all others, that particular being of hers now standing beside him, the borders of her body sharp, separate from the space outside, the lines made by her hand on the canvas creating their own special shapes and movement, the deliberate movement she had wrested from the jaws of the wills of others.

She looked around. They were alone, standing side by side, not touching, still separated by that hair's breadth as fine as air, so fine the lightest touch could have torn it away. But neither of them moved. They stood as still as two stone statues. Their eyes were motionless, as though they were terrified. Their skin was pale, as though the blood had drained from it.

It was like the fear we know in dreams, except that it was real. She was aware of its truth because her body trembled as she stood upright, and because of her sweating palms. Cautiously she moved one foot, then the other, beginning to move her body towards the door. But his body followed: 'Bahiah'.

She stopped, rooted to the ground for an instant, and answered faintly, 'Yes?'

'Where are you going?'

'I don't know.'

'Come with me.'

'Where to?'

Uncertainly, she realized that the regular sound of footsteps on the asphalt came from her own shoes. The sound was familiar, like her name ringing in the air. But her mind no longer trusted her ears. What sounded familiar to her ears became extremely strange to her mind. What had brought her feet to the asphalt of this street? She had never seen it before. It was not one of Cairo's usual flat streets which stretched on and could be seen right to the end. This street was not horizontal. It rose, like a road climbing a high mountain.

Astonished, she asked, 'Have we left Cairo?'

When she heard his voice beside her, she realized that she was not on her own and that the two of them had reached Qasr al-Aini street, passed through Fam al-Khaleej square and were now heading for Jebel al-Muqattam. She had never been there before. She had never walked up a mountain road, as she was doing now. Her life had always run on flat, horizontal lines. Her home was on the ground floor, and she entered it by climbing four steps. The tram took one or two steps. The dissecting room was on the ground floor, and the lecture hall was just three steps above the college grounds. The six steps leading to the laboratory were as high as she had ever climbed.

Now something strange began to happen to her body as she moved away from the earth. It became both heavier and lighter. It was as if she were shedding her body with every step, jettisoning the invisible weights that had hung from her wrists like heavy iron bracelets.

The sound of her shoes on the asphalt became less pronounced. Her feet moved independently — lightly — as if they no longer carried her body, or as if her body had become weightless. There was not a sound in the air around her. She clapped her hands together as she ran happily along: 'This is the first time I've ever climbed Jebel al-Muqattam.' She heard the echo of her voice from the foot of the mountain. She stopped and looked down. There was the great city, like a green carpet spread before her, with houses like tiny boxes. Her feet were inside her own familiar shoes, on the edge of the mountain. Near them another pair of feet stood inside an unfamiliar pair of black shoes.

She raised her eyes in astonishment and they met his. They were black, with a strange penetrating gaze that tore the mask from her face, stripped away the layers, making her visible.

She turned her head away and found nothing but the sky above and the bottomless abyss. She was overcome by that mysterious feeling that something momentous was about to happen to her: the chunk of brick underfoot would suddenly peel away from the mountain and her body would be drawn by the dreadful force of the earth and would shatter into little pieces, like particles. And just as in a dream, it seemed to her that had she jumped, her body would have torn loose from the earth's grip and soared into the sky. She stretched out one foot and nearly followed it with the other and jumped, but some mysterious force pulled her back. She thought it was his hand; but he was far from her, erect and motionless as a statue. His arms hung at his sides and his black eyes were firmly fixed on her, penetrating the long narrow corridor deep within her and seeing her profound secret depths. Then there was that rapid throb like the pulse of the universe in the night silence, and that mad rapid motion she had buried in the folds of her self and rolled up inside her, layer after layer, until it had become invisible and eternally secret.

The blood drained from her face and her fingers felt ice-cold. She closed her eyes with that deceptive movement she had learnt in her dreams. Then she opened them and realized that she was not dreaming and that the black eyes were still on hers. The blackness was not completely black; it was tinged with blue, a deep blue that spoke of unknown depths like the blue of the sky when we gaze at it and see that it does not exist, and the body trembles with awe at the immensity of the universe — a dreadful and terrible immensity silent and still, frightening not because of its real stillness, but because of its underlying motion, a violent motion of dazzling speed.

She hid her face in her hands and gasped almost inaudibly, 'Saleem'.

He answered in his low voice, 'Yes'.

'I'm afraid.'

'What of?'

'Of death.'

'Death does not exist . . . '

'But I'm afraid.'

'Of life then?'

'Yes.'

Anyone seeing her at that moment would have sensed that she was trembling. But her fear was not the kind that takes us away from danger; this was different, a fear that carries us closer to danger rather than further from it. It was a violent consuming desire to experience the peak of danger to its very end, that we might be rid of it for ever. This fear had weighed upon her heavily ever since she came to have a body of her own, separate from the world, wrenched from her mother's body as a small definite mass. The earth drew her downwards, the sky pulled her upwards, and the air pressed in from all sides. Her small body was always in the world's grip, caught between the lion's jaws. She was sure that someday the jaws would inevitably close. Had she ever doubted this, she might have considered some attempt at escape. But she bore her certainty within her body, in every throbbing cell, and she knew that the time would come and the pulse would stop. So sure was she that she longed for that moment, for the pulse to stop, relieving her of the burden.

She said faintly, 'Hold me with all your strength until . . . '

She stopped before she had finished the sentence. She had wanted to say 'until my pulse stops', but her secret death wish, once out in the open, would have seemed taboo and she understood why, for most people, the forbidden wishes are the real ones and the licit wishes unreal.

One move from him would have been enough to carry her to the end. But she had always been afraid of ends. She sensed the danger of arrival and realized the impossibility of going back where she had come from. She had always known that, in some magical way, she could become another person, someone other than

46

Bahiah Shaheen — she could become her real self.

She moved away from him, walking on ahead with her long, quick strides, her black eyes looking up. Their colour was just black enough, her nose upturned just enough, her skin pale from ill-concealed fear. She heard his voice from behind: 'Bahiah!'

She would not stop or answer. He shouted so loudly that his voice echoed from the mountain side:

'Bahiah!'

She began to run from the voice, but it came to her from every direction. She put her hands over her ears, but he pulled them away, shouting angrily, 'Why are you running away?'

She tried to move, but his arm blocked her way. She pushed at him with all her strength, but he pulled her towards him. He reached out, turned her face up, looked her straight in the eyes — angry eyes of black tinged with a terrible dark blue, like the blue of a bottomless sea. She tried to turn away but he stopped her, saying angrily, 'Bahiah Shaheen will always prevent you from attaining any goal. You will always stand in the middle of the road and fall into the trap of the mundane, like countless millions of others.'

His voice shook. He let go of her head and his hand fell trembling to her chest. Even her eyes were flickering. Everything in her life felt shaky. She had heard this trembling voice once, twice, many times, hundreds of times before — every day when she sat on the tram and watched the coined human pieces, when she saw the male students with their thick spectacles poring over their lecture notes, when she saw the female students with their legs stuck together, when she heard the lectures delivered in that monotonous drone, when the alarm clock assaulted her ears and when her father called her in that voice of his. Nothing could halt this monotony; it would continue for ever.

She was consumed by an overwhelming desire to stop this monotony which took possession of her constantly; a desire to shout, for no reason; to jump through the window and break an arm or a leg, to plunge a kitchen knife into her chest so that she would cry and hear her cries with her own ears and know for certain that she was alive and not dead. She had a strong and persistent desire to feel alive to the extent of committing a capital crime, a desire to kill her own body, while conscious and with full intent. She knew it would not have been a crime. There would be a crime only if her body was killed without her consent. She knew that another will was lying in wait for her, ready to seize the slightest opportunity to destroy her — her foot slipping on the tram step, a momentary distraction when crossing the street, a bullet tumbling randomly through the air.

To die in such a way, by chance and without her consent — that would really be a crime. But death would be legitimate if she were its deliberate target, if she were its choice and it hers.

When she looked up, she didn't see him. Turning quickly, she saw his back disappearing round a bend in the street. She shouted, 'Saleem!'

But there was no reply. She shouted louder, 'Saleem!'

Her quavering voice bounced back and forth off the mountain, but no one answered.

She stretched out on the bed in her small room. Her black eyes glittered in the dark like diamonds, absorbing the darkness and turning it into white rays of light. Millions of tiny particles floated in the rays, spinning in systematic circles, like the eternal motion of the universe, like the regular hum in her ear, and swept through her, down through her neck and legs, producing a light tickling sensation like the flow of blood through her hands and feet, gathering like pinheads at the tips of her fingers and toes. It was like the tiny feet of ants crawling under her skin and bones. She could almost hear their continuous faint buzz, like the millions of noises that make up the stillness of the night.

As she got up and her bare feet touched the cold floor, she lost her balance and would have fallen, had it not been for her strong legs and taut muscles, which kept her body straight. She pulled the canvas from behind the bed, turned the light onto it and sat on the floor on the small white mat, gazing at the cornelian-red particles floating in the light. As she squeezed her brush she felt pain, like the prick of needles. But her hand would not stop. It shuttled over the painting, with that deliberate movement, that urgent sweeping desire to experience the pain to the full, to press until her fingers bled and were crushed, putting an end to her pain.

A mysterious sweeping desire shook her body and seemed to stir the earth under her. It travelled from her fingers down through her arms, neck and head, as if along a taut electric wire, so that her fingers became stiff, her neck tense, and her head immobile.

Anyone seeing her at that moment would have thought she had been crucified. Were it not for the movement of her hand, she could have been thought to have died in her chair. But she was fully awake.

Her wide open eyes could detect the faintest of lines, even a dot. Her fingers could cut the black universe into two with the tip of her brush, making a white line, a hair's breadth, like the horizon separating the earth from the sky and day from night: a white line tinged with a dark deep red the colour of blood.

When she saw this deep red, her eyes widened, full of the dread of eyes before real blood. What was it about the colour of blood that frightened her? She gazed at the blue veins under her skin and felt the regular pulse in her wrist, one beat after the other. Some mysterious hidden feeling told her that the next beat would be the last and that the sound would stop, that she would breathe no more. She strained to listen. The final moment was still far off, but her ears could already detect it — faint and drawing nearer, just like the beat before and the next one, a continuous buzz that she fervently wished would cease. She strained to hear, waiting for the next beat and fearing that it would never come.

The alarm woke her in the morning. Her father's great eyes loomed over her bed, drawing her up, out of her room and out of the house. They followed her to the tram and the college. Then his thick palms shoved her into the dissecting room.

She stood on one foot alongside the marble table, lifting the other high as if to kick someone, then put it down with all its weight on the table's edge. A forbidden posture for man or woman. Dr Alawi, who would sweep past the tables in his white glasses and his short white coat, was the only man who could stand like that, alongside her table, one foot on the floor, the other balanced on the edge of the table next to hers. His blue eyes would be fixed on hers, but she never lowered her gaze. Her black eyes continued to look ahead, staring into space as if seeking something. They released millions of floating particles into the atmosphere. They probed the minute creatures drifting through the world, searching among the thousands of similar beings for the extraordinary face, for the eyes that would see her and make her visible — the black eyes that would pick her face out from among the others, and extricate her body from among the millions of bodies lost in the world.

But the faces were all the same, both in the dissecting room and out in the street. In the spacious but crowded college grounds, she felt as if she were drowning alone in a sea of people, unseen and unrecognized, and that her face had become like those of her fellow students. Bahiah, Aliah, Suad and Yvonne — it was all the same. Without thinking, she found herself fleeing the crowds, withdrawing to that small secluded corner opposite the college fence, behind the building. She sat on the wooden stool, leaning forwards, gazing at the tiny, palm-sized patch of earth where no green grass had ever grown. Unlike the earth around it, this furrowed patch was always mud-coloured, and between the ridges millions of tiny creatures, the size of ants, came and went.

'Bahiah . . . '

The name sounded as if it were someone else's and she jumped up from her stool. She saw the black eyes penetrating her own, tearing away their mask, stripping off the cover, penetrating the long narrow corridor, mercilessly and without hesitation, to her innermost depths. One brief moment more would be enough to reach the end.

But she called out faintly, 'Saleem.'

He remained silent, looking at her. 'Why did you leave me yesterday?' she asked.

His unflinching eyes fixed hers. She hid her face in her hands and cried.

'Why are you crying?' he asked her in a hushed tone.

'You don't love me enough.'

'You don't love anybody enough. You fear love like it was death — you're middle-of-the-road. That's Bahiah Shaheen for you.'

'No!' she shouted.

He handed her his white handkerchief to dry her tears. Her black eyes glistened in the sunlight and he smiled. 'What did you do last night?' he asked.

'Nothing.'

'Haven't you painted anything new?'

'No.'

He paused for a moment. Then: 'And what are you doing tonight?'

'I don't know', she whispered.

Reaching into his pocket, he drew out a small key. He handed it to her. 'This is the key to my flat in al-Muqattam', he said. 'Come any time after three. I'll be waiting for you.'

He vanished behind the college building. As she stood there, her fingers coiled around a small metal object with a rounded top and a hole in the middle. Its tail had small pointed teeth. As she ran her fingers over it, a shiver swept through her like particles of soft hot sand tingling in her hands, down through her legs, up through her head, along her neck and arms, and accumulating in the hand that gripped the small object.

It looked like the key to any other door. But she knew that objects change when feelings do. A little metal key can suddenly become magic, radiating heat that surges through the body like a burst of air and swells in the palm of the hand, filling it to overflowing.

She felt drops of sweat in her hot hand under the solid object, but when she ran her finger over its metal surface, she froze. Wrapping it in her handkerchief, she put it in her pocket and slipped through the crowded grounds, moving with a panther's long strides. She felt eyes staring at her, and slid her hand into her pocket to hide the key, as if, magical as it was, it might tear through handkerchief and pocket, leaping into view, as visible as the sun.

As she headed unthinkingly towards the college, her hand still thrust into her pocket, she heard a voice calling, 'Bahiah.'

She turned and saw Dr Alawi behind his white spectacles, surrounded by female students.

'Bahiah, where've you been?' he asked in his authoritative tone. 'I've been looking for you.'

Momentarily at a loss, she said, 'I've been in the girls' lounge.'

'Come to my room for five minutes', he said in a tone that bordered on command.

A female student whispered in her ear, 'He'll cane you with a ruler.'

Another laughed, clapping her hand over her mouth, 'He'll dissect you with his forceps.'

A third leaned forward and said, 'He'll tear you to pieces.'

A fourth sighed, 'Lucky you — I wish it was me!'

Moans, groans, sighs, and gasps, a hidden burning desire buried within her like a germ that sought to torture her body, rip it apart, destroy it so completely that nothing would remain.

She followed him into his office. He had already taken off his white coat and spectacles. The tension had gone out of the lecturer, who now stood as an athletic young man, slim and with a pale complexion, now reddish in the gleaming sunlight. His eyes were wider than usual, as if he was surprised: 'What's the matter with you these days, Bahiah? This is not the Bahiah we used to know.' She shuddered in panic, as if he had stripped off her clothes and glimpsed part of her so private that she had concealed it from others' eyes and kept it for herself alone. Pulling the collar of her blouse up around her neck, she said angrily, 'I'm the same as usual.'

He replied in the quiet tone of the confident lecturer, 'What about skipping your anatomy classes?'

'I was busy with the exhibition.'

'No, Bahiah. It's not the exhibition. You're busy with something else.'

Her lips parted in astonishment, but she pursed them quickly, as if angry. She turned to leave, but he blocked the way and continued to lecture her. 'You're busy with something else, Bahiah.'

She raised her eyes to his: 'No.'

As if he had not heard her reply, he asked in a quiet, confident voice, 'What's bothering you, Bahiah?'

'Nothing', she said again.

There was something between herself and Dr Alawi — something unspecified and incomprehensible but nevertheless real and palpable. She sensed it in his blue eyes when he looked at her, and in his voice when he spoke to her. Sometimes she wondered what it could be. She had seen him once in a dream. He was wearing a shirt and trousers and he was as slim as an athlete. His arm was hairy and looked reddish in the sunlight. He picked her up and tried to embrace her, but she slipped away. He put his arms round her, tore her hands from her mouth, and kissed her. She pushed him away, only to find there was no one there. She had been dreaming. She was surprised that Dr Alawi could force himself on her in her dreams, whereas she did not desire him when awake — on the contrary, she loathed him. She detested his piercing blue eyes and his laugh. He did not laugh like other people. His laugh was dignified and masterful. His guffaw was fake and abrupt. No sooner had it started than it was cut off. He always made people feel as if he was a lecturer, someone who knew what they did not and owned what they did not. He mounted the podium with steps like other lecturers: slow, self-confident, even relaxed. His bottom was a little flabby from sitting too long on comfortable chairs.

One of his hairy reddish hands was on the door knob, the other on her shoulder, patting it as teachers do their students. But now his hand rested there a moment, a quick touch like an involuntary contraction of the muscles. There was a slight tremor in his voice as he said, 'Bahiah, you know I care about you.'

He collected himself quickly, resuming his quiet confident lecturer's tone: 'Exams are coming up soon. And I want you to pass.'

At the tram stop she looked at her watch. Half past three. Her heart pounded. As she reached in her pocket, her fingertips found the hard metal edge. She withdrew her hand, shaking, as if she were carrying a bomb that would explode the moment she touched it, blowing her body to pieces on the asphalt. As the tram drew near, with its crowds and noise, she kept her distance from the others, so that no one would collide with her. Then she changed her mind and decided to walk home.

After Qasr al-Aini street, she headed for Nile Street. The sun shone on the river's surface, while the warm air caressed her face, bringing a light refreshing humidity. She closed her eyes under its warmth. The Corniche was deserted at that hour of the afternoon. The windows of the houses were closed, their shutters drawn, not a soul inside or out. The sounds of her footsteps on the asphalt rang in her ears with that familiar regular beat. But what sounded familiar to her ears seemed strange to her mind. The tapping on the asphalt came not from her own feet, but from others behind her. She turned, but there was no one. She felt almost disappointed, as if they had arranged to meet and he had not turned up. But she knew he was not behind her, that he was waiting for her in his flat at al-Muqattam, any time after three.

She glanced at her watch. Quarter to four. Her heart thumped and then stopped. Her black eyes looked up, her long thin face was pale and her short black hair fell over her neck and ears. Her delicate shoulders were softly rounded under her blouse. Her small breasts rose and fell with each breath and her red fingers clutched her leather satchel bulging with anatomy textbooks.

She came to Fam al-Khaleej Square. Before her was Nile Street and the bridge leading to her home in Rowdah. On her right was the Nile, on her left the road leading to al-Muqattam. Anyone seeing her would have expected her to turn left. But she did not. She remained standing where she was. She knew that to turn would be a matter of supreme importance. It would mean that she was Bahiah Shaheen no longer, that she had become that other, stronger being, equally desired and feared.

It was a dreadfully momentous time, which seemed like death. No, it *was* a kind of death — one person was dying and another being born — a brief moment if she would turn left. All she had to do was raise her foot, move it over the ground and bring it down again: no more than an instant, yet it seemed a lifetime to her, like all the years of her life so far and all the years she would have in the future, as if her whole life lay at her feet and she had only to step down and she would crush it to pulp, to soft ashes.

The street on her left was no longer a street. For streets, like everything else, change minute by minute according to our view of the world, the pulse in our veins, the change in the air with every new breath, and the surge of the sea with every wave. The street lengthened and protruded from the belly of the mountain like an outstretched arm. Above it, caught between the mountains and the buildings, a strip of sky formed a second arm. The two huge arms, like those of the mythical god, stretched out before her like the gaping jaws of fate, extending toward the horizon, lying in wait for her, willing her body to turn to them.

57

She longed to throw herself into those outstretched arms. But her body held fast and she was unable to lift her foot from the ground. She shuddered in panic and her satchel fell, the anatomy books scattering all over the road.

From the corner of her eye she saw the white label on the cover: Bahiah Shaheen, 1st Year Anatomy. Her arms seemed to shrink. They refused to pick up the books, but with her body still bent over the pavement she manged to gather them up and put them in her bag. Stooping over was enough to bring back Bahiah Shaheen full force. That other person disappeared down the long corridor and her feet quickly began to head towards home with determination.

As she walked her body's movement seemed strong and victorious, but her true feeling was entirely different. She felt defeated, and when she saw her house in the distance her heart sank, as though she were a lifer being led to prison, driven by an irresistible force as strong as steel. She felt chains around her hands, feet, wrists, ankles and neck, pulling her mercilessly towards that small red house.

Her home, her room and her bed were now no longer her own. Objects, like people, change not only in form but in meaning too. We never know the reality of things: we see only what we are aware of. It is our consciousness that determines the shape of the world around us — its size, motion and meaning.

She had thought of her home as a safe refuge from the crowds on the tram and at college, from the sun's heat and the winter cold, a place where her father would give her her daily pocket money, her mother would feed her, where her brothers' features mirrored her own. Everything around her evoked serenity. But now the house had become a prison, her father a guard, sitting on his bamboo chair watching her every movement, and trying to detect her secrets from her expression. Her personal papers in the drawers of her desk and under her pillow were covered with the prints of her mother's fingers, searching for her secrets, looking for love letters or her boyfriend's photograph. Her sisters' eyes besieged her with questions. Even worse were the almost daily visits of her uncle, his wife and their son — the business school graduate who since childhood had been picked as a potential suitor, with his silly smile and his murderous idiotic happiness.

Now she was sure that she did not belong to this family. The blood in her veins was not theirs. If blood was all that connected her to them, then she had to question that bond. She had to question the very blood that ran in her veins and theirs. Her mother had not given birth to her. Maybe she was a foundling, discovered outside the mosque. Even if her mother had conceived her — and whether or not her father had played a part in this — it did not mean that she belonged to them. Blood ties, she felt, were no bond at all, since they were no one's choice. It was pure chance that she was her mother and father's daughter; neither she nor they had chosen.

She did not know how she had arrived at this point of view, but she was sure of this one conclusion, that only human choice gives this bond any meaning. And from this she concluded something else: she wanted to establish some kind of bond with Saleem, something that would make him stop and come towards her when he saw her among thousands of others, something that would make her, alone among thousands, stop and come towards him. This deliberate movement towards him was the only thing that would give meaning to that bond, the only thing that would give her life meaning — otherwise what sense did it have?

She had had no clear purpose. She had never known exactly what she wanted from life. All she knew was that she did not want to be Bahiah Shaheen, nor be her mother and father's daughter; she did not want to go home or to college, and she did not want to be a doctor. She was not interested in money, nor did she long for a respectable husband, children, a house, a palace or anything like that. What did she want then?

Bahiah Shaheen's mind was not her own. But she had another mind. She could feel it in her head, a swelling thing that filled her skull, impishly and secretly telling her that all these things were worthless and that she wanted something else, something different, unknown but definite, specific yet undefined, something she could draw with the tip of her pen on the blank sheet of paper like an individual black line. But when she looked at it, it became a long line stretching as far and wide as the horizon, with no beginning and no end.

She wandered the streets like a lost soul. Like a particle of air lost among millions of others floating in a void, she surrendered herself to the wind and was blown back and forth. It may have seemed as if she had abandoned herself to the sensation of being lost, as though she relished her own dissolution and annihilation, but inwardly she resisted, tensing her muscles and fending off the random motion. She refused to submit to it; she forbade her feet to move; with all her might she fought to stop.

She found herself standing like a wild pony, her tall slim body erect, her black eyes looking up, her black hair falling over her forehead, ears and the nape of her neck. Her nose was straight and sharp, her lips pursed in anger. She looked round to see where she was. But she had never been here before. Nor had she ever seen the house, nor the people around her, who came and went in a never-ending stream. Nobody knew her and she knew no one. The blood pounded through her heart. Her breath came in great gulps as if she were drowning. Life around her had turned into permanent liquidity, water above and below, and her hands and feet found no solid purchase.

She reached out with shaking, panicky fingers as though thrashing in the water for a lifeline. When her hand touched the edge of her pocket, her fingers curled around the metal key and gripped it firmly, as if to make sure it was really there; its solidity seemed to reassure her that something in life was tangible, something could be grasped in the fingers.

With the speed and force of a drowning woman gripping a solid object, her body was driven, her feet strode steadily and quickly over the asphalt, and her eyes searched the jungle of streets for that protruding arm stretching between the horizon's heart and the blue sky caught between the buildings and the mountain. As she ran, she glanced at her watch: half past four. Her heart pounded and her chest rose and fell as her feet flew after each other, as if they were racing her breath.

A small door with a green branch of ivy hanging above it. As it opened, she saw his long, thin face with its deeply etched features, tense and exhausted. It was as if he never slept or ate, as if his head bore the world's burdens, as if his deep blue-black eyes with their penetrating gaze pierced all masks to reach inner depths.

'Hello, Bahiah.'

His voice surprised her. The name 'Bahiah' had acquired great intimacy. It was unlike any other Bahiah's name. It was hers to the exclusion of millions, she with her special being standing here on the west side of the room.

There was almost no furniture, just a big sofa in the corner, a table with a vase of roses, and the wide window with the towering mountain beyond. She sat on the sofa; he turned to close the door. His back was to her and she could no longer see his face, eyes or gestures. He seemed a stranger. When she heard the door close, she suddenly remembered that she was Bahiah Shaheen, hard-working, well-behaved medical student, and now she had turned up at the house of a strange man with a back just like other men and with no connection to her. She was amazed, as in a dream when you find yourself in a strange place for the first time, meeting strangers you have never met before.

Her brain started churning at dream speed, hurling up image after image. She imagined her father in his bamboo chair in the sitting room, sipping his morning coffee. He opens his newspaper, and finds that the naked body of his daughter Bahiah has been found in a bachelor's flat in al-Muqattam. Her father thought the road between home and the college delineated Bahiah's world, that she said her prayers, fasted, and studied four hours a day, that when a love song came over the radio she would turn it off, and that when any boy in the family teased her she would scold him. He thought she was unlike other girls, that her body was unlike others girls', in fact, that she had no body at all, no organs, especially no sexual organs liable to be aroused or stirred by someone of the opposite sex.

Her mind baulked at imagining her father's shock on seeing his polite, obedient daughter's body naked, not in her own bedroom but in a young man's flat. Not only he would see her, but so would thousands of others who read the morning paper, including the members of her vast family scattered across the country from Aswan to Alexandria (especially the peasants and the ones from Upper Egypt). Not to mention all the employees at the Ministry of Health: her father's superiors and subordinates, who had been convinced over thirty years that he was an efficient superintendent with close family ties and an honourable reputation, that his sons and daughters were diligent and well-behaved, especially his hard-working medical-student daughter Bahiah.

She shuddered as in a dream: she knew she would willingly sacrifice all the years of her life to spare her father that shock, that she did not mind dying or being seen naked if only her father would never see or know. She loved her father in spite of everything, and when he handed her an old ten-piastre note every day, her heart sank. When she folded her fingers around the note which carried the smell of his sweat, she wanted to bury her face in her hands and weep, for she knew that he worked so hard for her and her brothers and sisters. Sometimes she saw him pushing his way through the crowds with his thin body and bowed back; and when he crossed the street with its swirling traffic she would shiver with fear that a car might hit him. Once she saw him standing on the steps of the monstrously overcrowded tram and she imagined that the steps would collapse under the hundreds of feet and her father's body would be crushed under the wheels. Once she had been to her father's office at the Ministry of Health. She spotted him walking along the corridor behind his boss. His back was bowed, his neck muscles slack, and his head hung in submission, while his superior walked in front, his back straight, his neck muscles taut, his head tilted back arrogantly. She longed for the earth to swallow her up. Later when he sat near her on the tram and smiled, she did not smile back. She avoided his eyes until the next day, and when he handed her the sweaty, old note she nearly refused it. But finally she took it, feeling humiliated. When she managed to raise her eyes to his she saw an invisible, translucent tear.

As she jumped up he turned and there was his face directly before her, his eyes on hers. She was overwhelmed by that magical current, instantly felt that anything outside that moment was devoid of meaning and reality and that her whole life, past and present, was not really hers but belonged to some other person.

She had no connection with the world she had lived in, with the people she had known, or with anything other than this face, with its blue-black eyes fastened on her, asserting her existence.

'Saleem.

Her voice in the room sounded strange, like the voice of somebody else. So did the name 'Saleem' sound strange, like someone else's name. She repeated it several times in silence, to get used to its vibrations in her ears, and it sounded stranger every time. His name was Saleem and hers was Bahiah. His name sounded no stranger than her own. Names are so far from the reality of things. The senses are so hopeless in understanding feelings. What she felt for him went beyond the ability of her ears to hear, of her eyes to see, her nose to smell, and her fingers to touch. She realized that people have other senses, as yet undiscovered, that they lie latent in the inner self. But these other senses are more capable of feeling than the senses that are known to us. They are the real, natural senses, but they have never been developed by our upbringing, or by education, regulations, laws, traditions or indeed by anything at all. They are like a river flowing free without dams, or the rain pouring down from the sky, facing no barrier or obstacle until it is soaked up by the soil.

Now she sat on the sofa, he beside her, the window opposite and the mountain behind. Beyond the mountain the blue sky was tinged with the red glow of the late afternoon sun. The sunlight was reflected in her eyes like a radiant smile and she laughed with abandon, pointing to the window and saying, 'What a wonderful view!'

She expected him to take his eyes off her and look at the view, but he did not. His eyes remained on hers.

She stammered as she said, 'Why don't you look? Isn't the scenery wonderful?'

His eyes still on hers, he said, 'You are even more wonderful than the scenery!'

She looked away from him and he seemed surprised. 'Why do you look away?' he asked.

'I don't know', she replied, confused, 'but your eyes sometimes seem not to belong to you.'

'Whose eyes are they, then?'

'Someone else's.'

'Who do you prefer: him or me?'

'You.'

They both laughed. Then he asked, 'Do you want something to drink?'

'No.'

'Something to eat?'

'No.'

She laughed again, for no reason. When she heard the sound of her laughter she wondered whether this was happiness and whether happiness meant that the whole world with everyone and everything in it would disappear, leaving nothing but the small area of the sofa and its two adjacent bodies, not yet touching but divided by a space no greater than a millimetre.

She tried to retain that moment of happiness, to savour its taste. But it was thin and transparent, like a breath of air: if she raised her hand to touch it, it would be torn apart. Her hand was near his on the sofa a hair's breadth away, but neither of them moved so much as a finger. Both were afraid that if one of them moved, the hair's breadth of distance would die, and with it that fragile, veil-like moment of happiness.

But they were both frustrated by this moment. They wanted it driven to a conclusion: for no one can stand more than a moment of happiness, suspended in time like a floating particle of air, suspended, neither attracted by the earth nor drawn by the sky. How difficult it is for people to be suspended between earth and sky! How strong is their desire to put their feet on the ground, or on the surface of any solid object whose familiar weight reassures them that they really exist.

Like the force of gravity that attracts the body to the earth, his arms moved round her. They embraced with a violent desire to dissolve into the world, to lose all consciousness of the body and its weight, and to be annihilated and vanish in the air, like death, if you could manage to die and then come back to life and describe it. Yet it was not exactly like death, for in death people lose all feeling. It was like losing feeling yet not losing it, as though his body vanished while he was still there, and as though the world around him had been obliterated while he remained alive. As if the sky had become the earth and the earth the sky. It was all things intertwining, merging in a single point at the centre of the head, throbbing perceptibly like a heartbeat, but stronger.

She heard the violent pounding of his heart. It sounded like her own heartbeat. Everything of him that reached her senses became like the touch of her own body. Only with great difficulty could she distinguish her body from his: temperature, smell, complexion, the flow of blood in the veins — all were as similar as if they were in one body. She wanted to whisper something in his ear but she could not find the words. Would she say, 'I love you'? Before the words came to her lips, they seemed inadequate and fell far short of what she actually felt. What do the words 'I love you' mean?

Only silence could express what she really felt, because silence could convey something momentous: that words between people were no longer adequate, that she must coin new ones, a whole new language. He too was silent and absorbed, as if searching for the key to the moment of eternal contact when the body would no longer feel separated from the world but would become one with it, an enormous entity filling the space between sky and earth.

When she looked up and saw the mountain through the window-pane she slowly realized that she was returning to her definite position on the sofa. She ran her hand over her body and found that she had a body of her own, separate from his. Her eyes opened in astonishment, but she saw him in front of her and smiled. She laughed and said, 'Isn't this strange!'

'What is?'

'What's happening between us.'

'And what's happening between us?'

'Something strange.'

'Why so strange?'

'So fast, and without a word spoken!'

'In real life there's never any time and people invent words to justify their unreal lives.'

They both laughed.

'But how can we communicate with other people?' she asked.

'It's impossible to communicate with other people, Bahiah. People don't want a real person. They're used to faking everything, including themselves, and in the end they forget what their real selves are like. When they see a real person they panic and may even try to kill him. That's why such a person will always be hunted down, killed, condemned to death, imprisoned or isolated somewhere far from other people.'

'In a flat in al-Muqattam.'

'Yes, in a flat in al-Muqattam.'

'I love you, Saleem.'

His blue-black eyes were staring at the sky and the mountain and he was quiet for a long time, as if absorbed in something far off. She wanted to ask him: 'Do you love me, Saleem?' and to hear his voice saying, 'I love you, Bahiah.' But the question itself seemed meaningless, so what was the point of the answer? She loved him and whether or not he returned her love would change nothing in her feelings for him.

'What are you thinking about, Saleem?' she asked.

'In nine months we may have a baby.'

She shuddered. Her hand, lying on the arm of the sofa, began to shake and when she glanced at her watch she saw that it was half past seven. With a sinking feeling, she remembered her home, the college, her father, the dissecting room, her anatomy books, her fellow students, Dr Alawi, the tram, the streets, the people, and the whole world she had walked away from and to which she thought she would never return.

'A baby?' she asked in astonishment. The idea had never crossed her mind. She had never believed that children were created so fast and in such a trance, completely separated from earth and all sense of reality: can a body which dissolves in the universe create in that vanishing-point another body attached to the earth? Is it possible for a non-existent moment to create a concrete moment that can be touched and held?

She felt the new pulse deep within her like magical life born out of nothingness, as if a rock fixed firmly to a mountain suddenly moved and throbbed like a heartbeat. Her lips parted in astonishment and joy and she shouted, putting her hand on her belly, 'Look, Saleem, it's moving.'

He saw her looking at the mountain and asked in surprise, 'What is?'

'The mountain', she answered, laughing.

He laughed with her but she soon stopped, realizing that her joy was unreal: the mountain was not moving, nor the earth, the wall, the window, the sofa nor anything near her. All that was moving were the two hands on her wrist in their idiotic, slow, monotonous turn; they reminded her that time was ticking on and would never return, that the moments of her life were pouring into nothingness, and that nothing would remain but the absurd vibrations of two metal hands in a small metal box, piastre-sized and covered with glass.

'Saleem', she said sadly.

'Yes, Bahiah.'

'I don't want to go home.'

'Then don't go.'

'But . . . '

'But what?'

'My father, my mother, the people at the college and . . . '

'And Bahiah Shaheen . . . '

She felt droplets of sweat on her palm and under her armpits. Her complexion turned as pale as Bahiah Shaheen's, her eyes less dark and her nose less upturned. She tried to raise her head, to make her eyes as dark as they had been and to tilt her nose as sharply upwards, dividing the world into two, passing unhesitatingly through the middle, never fearing to reach the end, the end of the end. But by now Bahiah Shaheen had returned to her. How? She did not know.

70

Suddenly, without realizing what she was doing, she stood, took her bulging leather bag, and walked to the door.

Back in her bed that night, she felt that what had happened was only a dream. If not a dream, then an accident that had befallen her without her willing it, like all acts of fate and destiny. Somehow she was now back in her familiar bed, her body intact and with all its usual external boundaries.

But with some other mischievous part of her mind she realized that this accident was the only real thing in her life.It was not an accident, a dream, an act of fate and destiny or mere chance, but the only act she had ever performed intentionally, the only thing she had actually wanted to do.

None of her life was of her doing or her own choice. It was her mother who had given birth to her and her father who had enrolled her at the medical college. Her aunt, who suffered from a lung disease, wanted her to specialize in this particular field of medicine. Her uncle wanted her to be a successful, highly-paid doctor, who would marry his son, the business-school graduate. Her savings would grow thanks to his expertise in commerce, and they would raise children who would inherit their wealth and bear his name, and the names of his father and grandfather before him.

Everyone told her what they wanted. No one asked her what she wanted. In fact, she had never wanted any of the things they wanted for her. She did not want to be a doctor, and especially not a chest specialist. She used to watch the rows of TB patients looking like walking skeletons, their doctors obese and flabby. She had never liked her uncle or his son the businessman. The whole family thought him good-looking: he was tall, slim, with a fair complexion and pink cheeks. His eyes glowed with health and happiness. His features were as innocent as a child's. It was as if he was still being breast-fed. He gave everyone the same happy, vacuous smile.

She hated his smile and his happiness, and responded with bared teeth and angry lips. But he never got angry, believing — either because he was stupid or because, like all stupid men, he was arrogant — that she was hiding her real admiration for him behind those bared teeth. He would say to her in his dull, flat voice, 'I know women. A woman says no, but her heart says yes.'

She would have liked to spit in his face, but she would not do anything out of choice. So when she saw her father smiling at him, she would smile too, saying, 'Who told you that I'm a girl?' They were used to hearing this question from her. It did not annoy them; on the contrary, her father was rather pleased by it, as if secretly delighted that his daughter was not really a girl, or as if he wished, deep down, that she was not. She knew that her father's approval was genuine, for he had wanted her to be a boy. But her mother had willed something different and given birth to a girl — or perhaps it was not her mother at all, but mere chance that had made her female.

The word female sounded like an insult to her, like

73

the first exposed genitals she had ever seen. She felt embarrassed when she undressed in the bathroom. She could not stand to look at her naked body in the mirror. When her fingers approached her genitals while washing, she would jerk them away, as if her hand had touched an electrified or prohibited area. She still remembered the rap her mother gave her as a child. The traces of her mother's big fingers were engraved in her memory and stuck to her skin like a tattoo. Her mother's voice still rang in her ears: 'Don't do that. Say "I won't do it again!" ' She did not say it. What could there be in that forbidden area? She would examine her body with trembling hands. She felt that something dangerous was concealed in that forbidden place. She could not touch it or see it, but it was there all the same. She felt it clearly between her legs. Her mother's fingers would tremble when she neared it when she washed her daughter's body. It must be dangerous and frightening. But she carried it in her body as an inseparable part of her. Sometimes she would forget it and consider it one of the myths that had filled her head as a child. At other times it would become an inevitable naked truth like a live wire; when she touched it her body would shiver and tremble violently.

'Bahiah!' . . . Her father's voice rang in her ear like a shot, like the sole voice of truth. It made her realize that she was Bahiah Shaheen, hard-working, well-behaved medical student, the pure virgin, untouched by human hands and born without sex organs.

She pulled the bedclothes over her head and feigned sleep as she heard her father's footsteps coming toward the bed. His big fingers lifted the blankets and he stared at her and discovered, thunderstruck, that she was not Bahiah Shaheen after all: she was not his daughter, nor was she polite, obedient or a virgin; she had actually been born with sex organs, not only clearly visible through the bedclothes but moving as well, like the very heartbeat of life. By moving, she had removed the barrier in her way. She had torn away the membrane separating her from life. It was a thin membrane, intangible and invisible, like a transparent glass panel dividing her from her body, standing between herself and her reality. She could see herself through it but could not touch it or feel it, for it was like glass; the slightest movement and it would shatter.

Her mother used to gasp when she saw her jumping down the stairs. Then Bahiah would hear her heart thumping. She would tense the muscles of her legs, bring her thighs tightly together, and walk towards her mother with that familiar girl's gait: legs bound together, barely separated from one another. She felt that if they separated, something would tumble down like broken glass.

When her mother disappeared into the kitchen, Bahiah would go back to her jumping. It was not enough to bound down the stairs, so she would stand on the balcony (their flat was on the first floor) and leap, shouting for joy when she felt her body flying, weightless, as light as air. The earth would no longer pull her towards it, she had rid herself of its iron grip for ever — but it was a fleeting moment. She had time for just one joyful shout before gravity pulled her back and she tumbled down like a falling star, her body plummeting to the ground like a stone.

She would pick herself up, brush the dust off her clothes and gingerly touch her arms and legs. Everything was in place! Bones still unbroken. She then came to suspect that her mother had been lying to her and that no part of her was breakable after all. Then she would jump as she walked, swinging her legs freely and separating them wide apart, now certain that no glass object lay between them. She would climb onto the balcony and jump a second, third, fourth, and twentieth time. With each jump she became more convinced that nothing would break, that her muscles were strong and her bones firm. She pumped the air proudly with her knees, as her brother did when he walked. She stood erect, lifted her head high and focused on life, her dark eyes wide, sharp, and unblinking. With great pride she moved her feet over the ground. When standing, she would put one foot up on any chair or table. She would lift it onto any high edge, just like her father when he stood in the living room — and with the same pride.

'This is disgraceful, Bahiah', her mother said, slapping her knee to make her put her foot down. 'Can't you see how your girlfriends stand?' She would look at the other girl students with their fat, tightly bound legs, their beaten eyes like the eyes of the corpse laid out on the table, and their trembling lancets as they approached the uterus or penis. Their defeated eyes made her angry, and she was sure that she did not belong to this sex, that nothing in her was breakable. When she raised her eyes, her gaze was level, and no power on earth could make her lower them.

The next morning she went off to college as usual. She entered the dissecting room just like any other day, but she walked differently. Her feet were not hers. The hand holding the bag was not hers. Her eyes were no longer her own. She looked like the person who had been there yesterday, the day before and the day before that, but it was definitely not her. She was different. Things looked different to her. They were smaller and paler than before — and slower too. The bodies of the male students were smaller, the female students' legs moved more slowly. They walked like reptiles, legs together, and if their thighs happened to separate briefly, they would quickly snap together again. The girls pressed their legs together as if something valuable might fall if they separated. They held their leather satchels bulging with anatomy books against their chests, hiding something valuable from the male students' gaze and sharp elbows. None of the female students could walk alone. They always went in groups, like gaggles of geese. If one of them found herself alone in the college grounds or in the lecture hall she would quicken her step, her high heels tapping, anxious to catch up to the other women students and hide her body among theirs.

She saw Dr Alawi doing his rounds of the tables and sneaked out through the back door of the dissecting room. She wandered around the spacious grounds as if looking for someone, then went into the exhibition to look at the paintings and see her drawings. Her black eyes searched for those blue-black eyes, for the thin face with its exhausted, sharply-defined features. She left and walked slowly around the grounds scrutinizing the male students' faces. Their faces, movements and voices were all similar. When you looked into their eyes you would not even see them. She drowned in a sea, seen or recognized by no one. Her face became like those of the other female students: Bahiah, Aliah, Zakiah and Yvonne, it made no difference.

Without thinking, she ran out into the street. She recognized her footsteps. The street was not horizontal like all the others, but sloped upwards. Her body travelled up it and she panted as her eyes were drawn irresistibly to that grey cloud-coloured house; she was pulled by fine wires like invisible silken threads, with all the speed she could muster, in harmony with the blood coursing through her veins. The heat and warmth of her blood drove her on inexorably to her destiny, whatever it might be, even if it meant death and extinction.

With trembling fingers she slid the key into the lock and went in. As she stood in the empty room she could hear her own heartbeat; one breath followed the next in quick succession, as her chest heaved. 'Saleem!' she called out faintly, but the flat was empty.

She felt that dream-like amazement: the things we hold tight vanish in an instant, the body we embrace disappears in a flash, and when we open our eyes in the dark we see nothing but the wall and the bed beneath us.

She felt for what was beneath her and realized it was the sofa she had sat on the day before. She stretched out her arm in the dark and it hit the hard cold wall. She closed her eyes again and wondered if she was dreaming, but she was not. She knew Saleem was not there, that she was alone in his empty house, sitting wide awake on the sofa. She tried to make sure she was really awake but did not know how. All she could do was run her hand over her body, but she did that in dreams too when she was not sure if she was asleep or not. This frightened her, for she could not be sure of anything in her life. Any attempt to make certain would only add to her doubts.

When she opened her eyes in the morning she realized that she did not feel the familiar touch of her own bed. She saw the window and the mountain beyond it, and leapt up. It was the first night she had ever spent away from home, her first night in someone else's bed. She imagined her father bellowing like a bull after searching for her everywhere. She imagined her mother, sisters, uncles, aunts and everyone in the family fanning out across the world like locusts to look for her.

She walked heavily towards the mirror. It was obvious she had slept in her clothes; the whites of her eyes were tinged pink as if she had been crying or had stayed awake late into the night. She looked different from usual. She had always been a model girl, her clothes freshly pressed, the whites of her eyes clear, showing that she was a polite, obedient girl who slept in her own bed, had no worries and had never once cried in her entire life.

She had no idea where to go that morning, but her feet carried her to the medical college as usual. The grounds were crowded with students buzzing with unaccustomed activity. She fought her way through and headed for the dissecting room, but a male student stood in her way, saying, 'There's a strike today: no lectures, no dissecting room.'

She saw the other female students approaching with their bulging leather satchels and their closely-bound legs.

'Let's hurry home before public transport stops running', said one of the girls on hearing the news.

'Will it stop?'

'They say the tram and bus workers are coming out on strike too.'

'Why?'

'You ought to be ashamed . . . Don't you live on this planet?'

'They're just kids; it'll all be over soon and they'll go back to their notes.'

'Medical students don't care about anything but studying and memorizing their lectures. It's the law and arts students who know something about strikes!'

Questions and comments flew back and forth among the girls. Then: 'Let's go take a look', said one. But another pulled Bahiah towards the tram: 'Let's go home. The exam is only a month off.'

Shoulder to shoulder for support, they walked in a bunch towards the tram with their bowed heads and defeated eyes, their tightly-bound legs and their worm-like crawl.

Bahiah was now all alone, looking from afar at the crowd of male students as they assembled, trying to pick out that extraordinary face and those blue-black eyes that could see her and pick out her face from all the others. She leant against the wall, her bulging satchel dangling from her hand; her eyes looked up searching, her sharp, upturned nose divided the world in two and her lips were pursed in anger. She had never liked medical students, especially in big crowds. In her mind's eye she still saw them as they pushed into the lecture hall, with their thick glasses, bowed backs and sharp elbows, their eyes greedy for anything with the softness of flesh.

Suddenly the world seemed to rumble and shake as if an earthquake were rocking sky and earth. But she realized it was not an earthquake, but the sound of thousands of voices raised in unison: like the roar of thunder, like millions of voices melting into one enormous sound, filling the world, not merely reaching the ears but penetrating the pores of the skin and investing all the orifices of the body, spreading like gas and flowing like blood through the cells.

Minutes passed before she got used to the tremor and the sound. For the first time in her life she heard a slogan chanted by thousands of voices in one long, deep breath, as wide as the sky and as strong as a gale uprooting houses and trees. So great was the chorus that at first she could not make out the words of the slogan. Then the word 'Egypt' rang out. Not the 'Egypt' she was used to hearing from her father, mother, teacher, or fellow students, but 'Egypt' in that strong, mighty voice that filled the world and shook the earth and the skies. A shiver passed through her body and her hair stood on end. She felt a soft, warm motion under her eyelids like tears, and childhood images flashed before her eyes, rippling and dissolving as if under water: her mother's warm breast and

81

the smell of milk as she lay in her arms; the smell of dust and fig-trees in their village; her father's hand guiding her across the street; her aunt's long thin face as she coughed and spat blood; the eyes of her young brothers and sisters shut tight as they slept in a row, their open mouths drooling over the pillow; the hungry eyes of children along the canal; the lines of sick people in the hospital grounds; the wailing of women in their black, dusty clothes as they swarmed behind the corpse on its way out of the dissecting room.

She swallowed her tears and remained standing, her body still shivering and the great chorus still ringing out. The demonstration passed right by her. She saw faces different from those she knew from the dissecting room, bodies different from those she had seen forcing their way into the lecture hall. Their features were as sharp as swords, their complexions muddy, their backs straight and unbending, their eyes raised and their legs firm and rippling with muscles, as their feet strode over the earth, shaking sky and trees. She found herself with them and part of them, like part of an immense body with one heart and a single set of features. Her cheeks were rosy, her nose was sharp, dividing the world in two, her eyes stared straight ahead; she held her head high, her back straight and the muscles of her leg taut, while her footsteps shook the earth and her voice broke free from her throat, filling the world as she chanted with all her might, 'Egypt shall be free!'

She had the strange sensation of blending into the larger world, of becoming part of the infinite extended body of humanity, of dissolving like a drop of water in the sea or a particle of air in the atmosphere. It was a delicious, wonderful feeling, an overwhelming happiness as intoxicating for her body as the ecstasy she had experienced yesterday in that far-away place in the bosom of the mountain, or as a child when she saw the mythical god crushing something in his grip, then opening it and it was gone, or her childish laugh when her mother embraced her with all her might and their bodies would almost melt into one.

Her body had felt a hidden desire since childhood, since she developed a body of her own separate from the world. It was a persistent desire to return to the world, to dissolve to the last atom so that she would be liberated and disembodied and weightless, like a free spirit hovering without constraints of time or place and with no chains to tie her to earth.

It was a desire for the limitless, overwhelming freedom that comes only when you opt for salvation and destroys the hair's breadth that separates life from death — when you no longer fear death. When you have overcome the fear of death, you become capable of anything in life, including death itself.

At that moment she felt she could pierce iron with her body, take bullets and poisoned daggers in her chest, and that no power on earth could make her body fall, stop her legs from moving on, or prevent her voice from calling out for freedom. She was determined that there would be no going back; no power on earth could stand between her and her freedom.

And as if this decision had allowed her to relax, she let her body dissolve in the world, moving to its rhythm. Her steps were as a dancer's in a chorus. Her voice was not chanting a slogan, it was singing. The whole world was singing with her:

'My country, my country, I love you with all my heart.'

The sound came up from her lungs like warm

breaths. Under her ribs her heart pounded, her insides throbbed, and old wounds and past burdens left her body with each breath and heartbeat. Her eyes shed salty tears of joy that flowed down her cheeks and into her nose and mouth. As she licked the tears, she could not stop laughing and singing:

'My country, my country, I love you with all . . . '

The words 'I love you' were torn from her heart like a living part of her flesh, like her own warm blood. She shouted the words with all the strength she could muster, with all her suppressed desire to love and to fly as free as a bird in the sky.

Was it love that allowed her to understand all these feelings? She realized that it was. Real love makes us capable of loving everything and everyone; we open our arms to embrace the earth, the sky and the trees — only on opening our eyes do we realize that we are embracing a specific individual. The features and external boundaries are those we know by heart and which we could pick out from among the million bodies floating in the world; we recognize this particular individual with all his characteristics, and his eyes which can pick us out from among all other human beings.

These moments passed like a dream. All happy moments seem like a dream, and she awoke to the sound of gunfire. It was this sound that brought her back to the reality of her life and to the chains that tied her to the earth. The more bullets rang out, the more aware of the truth she became. She saw some students fall to the ground. Others advanced, facing the bullets head on, while still others sought protection in the doorways of houses and shops.

She stood still as a statue, her black eyes gazing up. Had a bullet been aimed at her body, she would have been killed immediately, but she knew she could not die against her will. She did not want to die yet: but she wanted to cry. Sadness was the only truth in her life. Before she had laughed without really wanting to; when she had been happy she had always had the inner conviction that this happiness was not real and that something threatened her, threatened her very life. Another will was always lying in wait for her, lurking round every corner, waiting for an opportunity to attack her when there was no one to rescue her, neither her father nor mother, brothers nor sisters. No one at all.

Suddenly, as if it had surged from the depths of the earth, she saw Saleem's face. He was kneeling to lift a bleeding body. All the images vanished from her eyes. Only that face with its distinct features remained as he slowly crossed the square, carrying a body: the head lolled and the white shirt was soaked with red blood, leaving a long red trail on the asphalt behind them.

She sat in the room adjacent to the operating theatre at the old Qasr al-Aini Hospital as if in a trance, suspended between belief and disbelief. She could not believe that so much had happened in so short a time. But Saleem's blue-black eyes attested to her existence and the fact that she was not dreaming. When he disappeared into the adjoining room, things around her would lose existence and reality. When he returned and their eyes met, a strange feeling of the truth of things and of existence coursed through her body. Then she realized that this moment was her real age, that all past days and years were no more than dream or illusion.

Her mouth felt the true taste of life: hot and biting, mixed with the penetrating smell of ether and iodine. A noticeable shiver ran down her ribs, her hand trembled when she touched anything and her legs shook when she stood or walked: it was the tremor of real life, a mixture of fear and bravery, a sense of both danger and safety, a loss of time and place and yet the acquisition of a remarkable ability to experience them both. It was a heady mixture of contradictory feelings, melting in complete harmony like the colours of a rainbow.

She thought that the entire world must be in motion to provoke this strange mixture of feelings in her body: the strike, the demonstration, the chanted slogans, the anthem, the bullets, the falling bodies, the red blood flowing on the ground, the bleeding body she had helped to carry into the car, the operating theatre, the smell of ether and iodine, the doctors in their white gowns and the nurses in their white caps — it was all this that created that contradictory mixture of sensations in her body.

She felt a profound hidden sadness overlaid by a strange overwhelming happiness, evident as a glimmer in her black eyes, like a swift movement, a breath of hot air, like a child panting after a ball or a sparrow's wings flapping in the sun. She heard one of the doctors say, 'Magdi's dead.'

His voice was as penetrating as another bullet, tearing through her and separating waking from dreaming, life from death. She found that seven students had died and many more were wounded, that others had been driven off to prison, and that Egypt was not free. The chains were still there, the hungry-eyed children still lived beside the canal, the columns of patients still stood in the hospital grounds spitting blood, the women in black still cried and wailed, her father still sat in his bamboo chair in the living room, and the policeman was still in his wooden shelter on the corner sniffing blood.

Her head slumped on her chest as if she was sleeping. She must really have slept because she woke to the sound of Saleem's voice, and when he called her everything seemed like a dream: 'Bahiah . . . '

She leapt from her chair. 'Bahiah': he had picked her name among all others, recognized her face among all others, and headed towards her with his deliberate stride. Then there was his distinctive voice, 'Bahiah, you're exhausted. Your clothes are all blood-stained.' She looked down and saw bloodstains on her chest and sleeves. It was Magdi's blood, which had dried in his veins just a few minutes ago. Dr Fawzi said: 'Saleem, your shirt is soaked with blood. Come along to the doctors' canteen so we can clean you up.'

The doctors' canteen was in New Qasr al-Aini street, so they crossed the small bridge leading from the old hospital to the new. The water flowed fast under the bridge, and a young couple in a rowboat laughed and waved to a blonde woman standing on the balcony of one of the Garden City palaces. The usual crowd had gathered at the hospital gates. Animals pulled carts laden with oranges. There were people with skinny faces and bodies like skeletons, women carrying children with the faces of old people, and old people with the bodies of children. There were women with men's features and men with women's features. On the asphalt was blood, spittle and children's excrement; scabrous, hungry dogs rummaged in the garbage scattered here and there.

A car hooted sharply behind them. Four fat faces and eight staring eyes in a big black car. 'Police', Saleem whispered.

A man with a long tapering mouth like a rat approached them and said, 'Come with me.'

No one moved and three men surrounded them and led them to a big box-like car: it was closed on all sides and dark as a prison cell inside.

She sat near a keyhole-sized crack in the side of the car. Through it she saw the streets with their crowds, cars and trams. It was almost sunset. Streets, houses and shops began to light up. People were just coming out for a stroll, a night-shift or a trip to the shops. The world was different when viewed through a small hole in a closed box. It was like the enchanted world she used to see as a child through magic lanterns or in magic tricks.

The churning in the streets and the people's actions seemed odd to her, divorced from the world she now inhabited, a world that seemed to know nothing of food, drink, sleep, homes, fathers, mothers, shops, shoppers, new-born children, dying old people, and streets for people to walk on or rails for trams to run on. People's movements as they walked seemed absurd and meaningless. She imagined that they were dead or lived in a passive world without warmth or pulse. The world of other people appeared dead to her. Her whole life was focused on that car like a closed box, or more specifically on the seat occupied by that slim body, with its exhausted head and burdened features, its deep eyes with their strange ability to see and penetrate to the reality of things.

The car stopped, the door of the box opened. Several men arrived. Walking ahead of and behind them, they took them into a strange building and she found herself in a small empty room. The door closed behind her, and she was alone. She stared at the closed door, seeing nothing else. A wide barrier of thick, dark wood separated her from Saleem; it stood between her and life, preventing her from moving and thwarting her will — like her mother's big arms when they pulled her towards her, her mother's voice scolding her, the sound of the tram as it crawled along the rails, the iron gate of the college, the dissecting room with its marble tables covered with the remains of corpses, the crooked legs of the male students, the beaten eyes of the female students and Dr Alawi's blue eyes with their hidden greed.

She pounded the massive wooden door with her strong fist. She kicked it with both feet, hit it with her entire body; she bounced back and hit the wall, then threw herself at the door again. It was like someone banging against a wall and splitting open his head instead of bringing down the wall. But her head did not split. Nothing in her would break. Her body lay stretched out on the ground, taking up the space between the wall and the door. Trickles of blood ran down from her nose and ears and between her fingers and toes. A policeman opened the door, his nose sniffing the blood, his eyes spying. She stared at him with her black eyes and then looked down submissively, but like all policemen, he countered that move with arrogance, tensing the muscles of his back and neck. His eyes bulged like those of a man who had been hanged and a whip dangled from his thick, gnarled, hangman's fingers.

Everything around her seemed familiar, as if it had all happened before. She had experienced the pain in her body before; she had seen these red spots on the ground and this same policeman before: the eyes, the nose, the whip, the wall, the red spots, the door — everything repeated itself. It was as if she could foretell what would happen tomorrow. She hid the white sheet of paper under the straw mat as she used to hide it from her father. When the guard disappeared she took it out again. She looked at her distinctive lines. She could recognize them as easily as she could recognize her own features. With that strong deliberate movement, she drew her brush over the blank sheet of paper. Everything took on a new form and new colours. She had discovered the true colours of things. Her eyes saw that the leaves of the trees were not green, the sky not blue, the wall not grey — indeed, it was as transparent as a silk curtain. Her body could penetrate it easily. She felt a strange power, not illusory but real, with a tangible material density. She felt it with her fingers, strong and flexible as rubber. She would not break, merely bend under pressure. She knew that her body could not withdraw from life. Her heart would continue to pound in ever faster bursts. Everything took on a splendid, radiant colour. The red spots on the floor shined like the sun, the stars burned as brightly as the moon. The green of the trees turned dark blue. The veins and texture of each leaf were as prominent as chattering teeth and the air shook them with an invisible vibration like the motion of time. The past merged with the present and future. Yesterday was today and the day after. Time ceased to exist. Only in a prison cell can this glorious truth be discovered.

This discovery was the real reason behind the strange ecstasy that now appeared in her black eyes, and which made her bleeding body dance with a rare agility and toy with the hordes of bedbugs swarming over the straw mat. The body acquires this extraordinary ability when it rids itself of its false human consciousness and achieves true awareness.

The prison guard was surprised when he peered through the door. Bahiah was holding out her arm and running her hand over her swollen veins. When she felt the blood coursing through her body she laughed: for thousands of years people had tried to unravel the mysteries of blood circulation. She looked at the policeman with her black eyes. She now understood that the world revolved in time with the circulation of blood in her body; it was this circulation itself that frightened policemen and paralysed their thinking, especially if the circulation was so powerful that the surface became smooth and still like the surface of the earth — though it was blood-red and flowed slow and proud through the blue veins under the skin.

The policeman asked in a sharp, effeminate voice: 'Are you Bahiah Shaheen?'

Still laughing, she looked up with her usual arrogance and replied 'No!'

The policeman stared at her with bulging eyes, 'Are you lying?'

She laughed, snapping her fingers. He slapped her face. Thin red streaks ran from her mouth and nose, but her black eyes were still upturned and her nose kept its sharp upward tilt, dividing the world in two. When she walked alongside the policeman, her legs seemed long in their black trousers. Her muscles were taut, her bones straight; with each stride she hit the ground distinctly, separating her legs confidently. When she reached the large room crowded with people, she assumed her usual stance: her weight on her right foot, she lifted her left foot high and propped it on the wooden barrier that separated her from an officer seated behind a small desk.

The officer opened a large book the size of his desk top and his voice rang out: 'Bahiah Shaheen!'

She realized he was calling someone else, so she did not reply. But he called out once more, still louder: 'Bahiah Shaheen!'

She looked around, searching among the faces for someone called Bahiah Shaheen. She could not recognize her face among the women standing or sitting on the floor. A long, feminine laugh rang out, followed by giggling and the popping of chewing gum; kisses were blown, and the smell of sweat and dirt mixed with an overpowering odour like iodine; some faces were fat and chubby and others were just skin and bone. On some faces the black eye-shadow had melted in the heat and formed a smudgy black ring around the eyes. A plump, flabby body revealed its curves under a tight silk dress that clung to the lines of breast and bottom. There was also a skinny body like a dried corn-stalk, with no breasts or bottom. Small feminine feet with long, red nails and cracked heels darkened with mud poked out from open slippers.

One of the skinny ones said, 'Where's Bahiah Shaheen?'

'A fat one answered, 'I'm Bahiah al-Sharbatali.'

'Welcome!'

'Thank you.'

'When will God have mercy on us?'

'God is pleased with us all right.'

'Really?'

'Sure, we're the best of women.'

'I feel better now.'

'Without us honourable husbands would have died and respectable households might have collapsed.'

'But they hate our smell . . . '

'Because it's their real smell.'

'And they put us in prison.'

'Because we know what their genitals look like.'

93

'They're scared to death of us.'

'And they die of desire for us.'

The long, drawn-out laughs, the clacking of slippers and the popping of chewing gum went on. The smell of perfumed filth filled the air. The officer thumped his hand on the colourless desk which looked like a kitchen work-table and shouted angrily, 'Shut up, gypsies! Where are your manners?'

One of the women giggled: 'What manners, sergeant! The people with manners are all dead.'

He winked at her, 'You got that right.'

Then he glanced at her with threatening eyes shining with lust.

Bahiah's lips parted in a smile, which died when she saw her father, who seemed to have emerged from the depths of the earth. He gave her a sharp, threatening look as he answered the officer's questions, scribbled his signature on the investigation record, paid ten Egyptian pounds and took his daughter away.

She got into the taxi. Her father sat on her right, her uncle on her left. The door shut and the taxi moved off. It was as if she had been arrested again, but this time by another kind of police. Her father on one side and her uncle on the other seemed like policemen. Their faces, in profile, were immobile. They stared straight ahead, avoiding her eyes; they were like two strange policemen to her, taking her to the guillotine or a prison cell.

All the men of the family met. They sat round the table devouring stuffed chicken. After lunch they sat smoking in the hall, picking their teeth with toothpicks; their bellies swelled over their thighs like pregnant women and their fat, flabby bottoms filled the big bamboo chairs. Each would belch audibly, clear

94

his throat and say something in a coarse, deep voice that was not his own. 'In my opinion, we should take her out of school. Universities corrupt girls' morals.'

Another replied, 'I think we should marry her off as soon as possible: marriage is the strongest protection for girls' morals.'

A third said, 'It's my opinion that we should do both: take her out of medical school *and* marry her off. We already have a groom.'

She was in the grip of fate. Iron fingers held her relentlessly. The bars were so close together that she could not even poke her head out. Fate was her father, who owned her just as he owned his underwear. He might or might not educate her, for he was the one who paid the fees. He could marry her off or not marry her off, for he was the broker, even though she had never authorized him.

A conspiracy was woven against her in great secrecy. She heard whispers. She saw the look in their eyes. She sensed the impending danger and looked for a way out. At midnight, when she heard her father's snores, she sneaked out of her bed, dressed, and sat on the edge of her bed wondering where to go. Where could a girl of eighteen like her go at this time of night?

She had never felt that she was a girl or that she was eighteen. This used to be called the age of puberty. A suspicious word. At the mere sound of it fathers and mothers tremble with suppressed sexual desire, baring their teeth and shaking a warning finger at their sons and daughters. Other eyes look at them suspiciously, but mothers and fathers follow their own instincts free from suspicion.

She knew they would interpret her escape from home in sexual terms alone, although at the time she had no sexual desire at all (her relationship with Saleem was something different). Since the time her mother had smacked her when she was three, she felt disgusted by the sight of sexual organs in the bathroom, and would quickly avert her eyes. She was not even aware of being female. She did not consider Saleem male. She saw her real self in his eyes. Going to him was an assertion of her freedom and choice. When she was with him, she lost all desire for food as well as her sexual appetite. She would become a human being without instincts and without those familiar desires. She would be in the grip of a new, wild, nameless desire: the desire to be her real self and to trample all other wills down with hers, to tear her birth certificate to pieces, to change her name, to change her father and mother, to gouge out the eyes of those who had cheated and deceived her, including herself, so that no one would be able to take her own eyes and replace them with eyes that were not hers.

She had always known that her eyes lied and that they hid her sexual desires, but not by choice. Her sexual desire was shrinking despite her. She could feel it withdrawing from her, leaving her body on its own. Sometimes when she felt the need for it she would try to summon it up, but it refused to respond and never settled in her body. The cries of her sister Fawziah still rang in her ears: there was a red pool of blood under her. Every day she waited for her turn. The door would open and Umm Muhammad would enter with the sharp razor in her hand, ready to cut that small thing between her thighs. But Umm Muhammad died and her father was transferred to Cairo and that small thing between her thighs remained intact.

Sometimes she was afraid of it, thinking that it was harmful, that it had been forgotten or left inside her body by mistake. She would long for Umm Muhammad to rise from her grave and come with her razor. But the image of her sister Fawziah, limping and moaning as she walked, would flash through her mind. When the wound healed Fawziah could no longer run as she used to. Her steps became slower and when she walked her legs remained bound together: one leg would not dare to part from the other.

Bahiah came to hate bath-days. When she undressed she looked with loathing at her sexual organs. She even hated God for creating them. She had once heard her father say that it was God who created our bodies and sexual organs. One day she told her mother that she hated God. Her mother gasped and slapped her face: 'How can you say such a thing?'

In tears, she replied, 'Because he's created bad things.'

Her mother hit her again, saying, 'God creates only beautiful things.'

'But who created those bad organs?'

Her mother looked at her wide-eyed and did not reply. That night she heard her whispering to her father, 'The girl is not normal.'

Since she did not know what was normal, she imagined that sexual desire was abnormal. So she was disgusted when she saw men's sexual organs bulging under their trousers; she wanted to throw up when a man dug his elbow into her chest as she waited for the tram. She hated men with their trousers, their ugly protruding organs, their greedy, shifty eyes, their smell of onions and tobacco, and their thick moustaches which looked like black, dead insects flapping over their lips.

She knew that her father was a man and so she hated him all the more. At night when his snoring stopped she would imagine that he had died. She did not love her mother, nor did she love women with their low-cut dresses, revealing breasts swollen with hidden desire, and their eyes made up with kohl, like slave maidens burning with lust. But their flat, closely-bound legs and their beaten eyes betrayed their ever-lasting frigidity.

But to them she was an adolescent. When she stood on the balcony to enjoy the sun her father would imagine that she was within sight of their bald neighbour. If she was late, absent-minded, drawing, thinking, having a bath, or looking in the mirror, the reason was all too obvious: a man. She later realized that parents thought of nothing but sex and imagined that their offspring were just like them.

At a big family party they sold her to a man for three hundred Egyptian pounds. Musical instruments played, dancers' bodies shook, men's eyes glowed with lust and bellies were filled with food and drink. Her face was surrounded by flowers and lights but it looked pale. Her mother made shrill cries of joy in a sharp voice that was stifled just at the end, like a suppressed sob. Her father paced up and down in his new suit. From time to time he put his hand in his pocket, feeling for his wallet, bulging with money for her dowry. Children were playing and running about, but whenever their eyes fell on the bride they touched their genitals under their clothes in fear. Men walked about in their trousers, their bent legs striding back and forth, exhibiting a flabby and insatiable virility. Women wore their shiniest dresses, and their soft eyes were veiled by memories of sad weddings.

Her white silk dress stretched tightly over her chest, smothering her breasts. A long tail folded like a coffin around her bottom and legs, and dragged along for her feet, uncomfortable in elegant high heels, to trip over. The bridal stage, surrounded by roses, looked like the grave of the unknown soldier. The drums' slow, heavy beat sounded funereal strains. Her small cold hand lay in the bridegroom's large palm. His fingers were strange. They coiled around hers like the fingers of fate. Under the folds of the coffin her legs moved slowly as if she was heading for unknown disaster. Her black eyes were open, gazing forwards, unfocused.

She heard the door slam violently. All noise ceased and the images faded. She found herself sitting in what looked like a police car. On her right was a man, her father; on her left was another, the bridegroom. Their faces in profile were taut. Their muscles too. Their eyes stared ahead, secretly watching her, like a policeman's.

At the door to the new flat, the father handed over his property to the bridegroom: Bahiah Shaheen passed from the hands of Muhammad Shaheen into the hands of Muhammad Yaseen. But neither of the two men yet realized that she was Bahiah Shaheen, and consequently could not be Bahiah Yaseen.

She was the only one who knew. When the door closed behind them she raised her defiant eyes and saw a black moustache topped by a white spot the colour of snot. She saw his sweaty, thick, black chest hairs and the jungle of hair on his lower stomach. When he jumped into bed like a monkey, she laughed audibly and his eyes widened in astonishment. But when she walked slowly towards the wardrobe and opened it, she was astonished too.

She found nightdresses with cut-away fronts, backs and bellies, kinky underwear, perfumes, red, white and green bottles of make-up, eye brushes, slippers with red roses on them, hand towels, toilet soap, hair-removing cream, deodorants, and massage and body oils. Women's tools in their married life are all sexual. A girl moves from her father's house to a husband's and suddenly changes from a non-sexual being with no sexual organs to a sexual creature who sleeps, wakes, eats and drinks sex. With amazing stupidity, they think that those parts that have been cut away can somehow return, and that murdered, dead, and satiated desire can be revived.

He smiled proudly to himself, thinking that her rejection was typical of a virgin who has no knowledge of men. Her ignorance gave him the self-confidence to parade naked before her, exhibiting his virility. She laughed again and his male aggressiveness was aroused, so he attacked her like a ravenous beast. She kicked him in the stomach and he fell to the floor, wiping his eyes in surprise and disbelief. This strong foot could not possibly belong to a female. For a female's foot, from his experience with prostitutes, was so soft and small that he could bend it with one hand. But this foot was as firm and strong as a bullet.

He told himself that a wife was not the same as a prostitute. He assumed that the strength of a virgin's rejection would increase in direct proportion to her purity and ignorance of the male. His arrogance mounted: he was now certain that he was the first invader. He felt sure that she would not discover his weakness so he attacked her more violently. She merely kicked him all the harder.

Despite his sluggish husband's mind, it began to

dawn on him that she was rejecting him. His eyes widened in horror and he asked angrily, 'What makes you refuse?'

She answered even more angrily, 'I'm not a prostitute.'

'You're my wife', he said in his owner's voice.

'Who said so?' she asked in astonishment.

'Your father, myself and the marriage broker.'

'That must be the basest deal in history!' she shouted angrily.

He slapped her face and she laughed. She realized that people get angry when we uncover their disgraceful secrets. He was naked. His genitals were black and ugly. She glanced at them in disgust.

He hid the lower part of his body under the sheet, like a shy virgin on her wedding night. But then he remembered that he was a man and a man is not supposed to be shy, so he tore the sheet away and looked at her. Her black upturned eyes did not waver.

He shouted angrily, 'You're not a woman.'

The traditional insult a man hurls at a woman, believing that it will cause the earth to tremble under her and that she will be left with nothing. What could possibly be left to a woman if she does not worship men's genitals?

She shrugged her shoulders and said, 'Anyway, who told you that I'm a woman?'

'Your father must have tricked me then', he said angrily.

'You should get your money back', she laughed.

'He's a con man.'

'You should have examined the cow before you bought it.'

She was trying to create a scandal, for scandal alone could save her now, could make everyone cast her out.

She wanted to be cast out, to have no mother or father, and no family to protect her. For protection itself was the real danger: it was an assault on her reality, the usurpation of her will and of her very existence.

She sat in the chair and finally saw him pull up the sheet and fall asleep. His snoring gradually grew louder and she realized that a husband's snores are like a father's. She tiptoed out into the street. When she saw the red morning glow she realized that it was now the 'day after'. Scandal awaited the whole family: her father would come looking for blood, her mother would inspect the sheets and nightdresses, and members of the family would be all over the newly-weds' house searching in vain for the family's non-existent honour.

She strode confidently along the street in her white blouse and black trousers, taking long, quick steps like an athlete. She wore flat-heeled shoes; her short black hair fell over her ears and the nape of her neck. Her eyes were dark as she looked up. Her sharp up-turned nose cut the world in two mercilessly and without hesitation. Her lips were pursed in determination and anger. When she reached Qasr al-Aini street she knew where she was going.

She saw one of the female students getting off the tram, and she hid behind a wall. She watched the groups of students getting off the bus and tram and walking towards the college. When the street emptied and the college had swallowed up the students, she left her hiding place and walked around the college fence. Through the iron railings she saw the door of the dissecting room. The door next to it still bore a white label with her name on it. She could see students' heads moving behind the windows of lecture halls and the dissecting room.

'Bahiah Shaheen!'

The voice rang out behind her and she jumped. One of her fellow students stood before her. She remembered his name. It was Raouf Qadri.

'How's college?' he asked.

'I never went back.'

'So they've kicked you out too?'

'Why, who was kicked out?'

'Four so far. And I'm the fifth.'

'I was kicked out too, but by a different authority.'

He laughed. 'Well, there are all kinds of authorities, but kicked out is kicked out.'

'What about Dr Fawzi?' she asked.

'He's in the hospital as usual.'

She crossed the small bridge between the old and new hospitals. Through railings she saw the decorated boat and the couple waving to the woman standing on the palace balcony.

A big black car drove by. It looked like a police car. It was followed by an ambulance which, with its deafening siren, fought its way through the crowds standing in front of the hospital. There were queues of pale-faced men, women in black gallabiahs, children with bulging eyes, orange peddlers with their animal-drawn carts. Cats and dogs scampered among the piles of rubbish.

She entered the grounds of the spacious new hospital. Cars belonging to college lecturers and doctors were lined up like great ships moored in a port or aircraft waiting on a runway. Their curved tops shone like steel under the sun's rays. Their bonnets were sharp and pointed like gun muzzles, their rear ends long and soft like snake tails. She stamped her foot hard on the ground, as if she were stamping on all those soft tails and sharp pointed heads, on all lecturers and doctors with their great shiny cars, bulging stomachs and flabby bottoms, their comfortable leather seats, their names hanging from signs in squares and streets, the diplomas they flaunted and the smell of blood and patients' sweat oozing from the paper money lining their fat pockets.

She headed towards the out-patients' department and saw Dr Fawzi's head bobbing over the queue of bodies as skinny as skeletons. People leaned on each other for support. Thin, crooked legs unbent and straightened up. A head held itself erect with difficulty. Eyes were hollow, mouths open and panting, and a vile corpse-like smell filled the air.

She fought her way through the crowds to reach Dr Fawzi — although 'fought her way' is perhaps the wrong expression, for no sooner had she touched a body than it would stagger, lean against the wall or fall onto another. Yellow eyes strained towards her, seeing her as if from behind a cloud or from another world. In a daze, they realized they were standing in a queue.

Dr Fawzi was sitting at the head of the queue, his metal stethoscope hanging round his neck like a gallows rope. With his pen he wrote the names of mixtures. Sweat poured from his forehead as his voice rang out above the panting breaths, rattling throats and rasping coughs: 'Breathe in! Hold your breath! Say ah . . . ! Say one, two, three, four! Stretch out your hand! Stretch out your leg! Pull yourself together!'

When Dr Fawzi saw her standing there he left his seat and came up to her smiling. 'Hello, Bahiah', he said. 'I wanted to get in touch with you to see if you were all right, but I didn't have your address. Are you all right?'

'No', she said softly.

Their eyes met in a long moment of silence. 'How's Saleem?' she asked.

'They've moved him from Misr prison to Torrah prison.'

'Any visitors allowed?'

'No, not even his mother.'

'I heard they've released some of the students.'

'That may be true . . . but no one like Saleem will be released now.'

'When, then?'

'No one knows. It might be years.'

'Years?' she shouted.

'Yes, I'm afraid so', he said sadly. 'Nobody knows how long.'

She shook his hand with frightened fingers and ran out into the street. She saw people going to work or going home as if nothing important had happened. The most momentous possible thing had happened and no one knew or cared. She wandered the streets aimlessly. When she reached the college fence she looked up at the windows and saw the students' heads as they bent over the corpses. They looked just like they did on any other day, as if nothing had happened. She growled in anger and stamped the ground. How ugly ordinary life was after a great event!

How awful that life went on heedlessly! The sky remained suspended on high, the earth stretched out below; the clouds moved with their usual nonchalance and people walked in the streets with their usual indifference. Would such frivolity never cease? Again she stamped her foot. Why wouldn't this indifferent motion stop its grinding cycle? Why wouldn't people stop for a moment, wake up and see the iron chains around their necks?

'Bahiah!'

She jumped as she heard the voice behind her.

A face peered out of a big black car like a police vehicle. She recognized the face immediately. Dr Alawi. He got out, came up to her and said eagerly, 'Bahiah! Where've you been all this time?'

She was silent. He took her hand and pulled her to the car. 'Come with me!' he said. 'I want to talk to you!'

It was noon. The sun shone brightly through the car window, she could feel its heat on her arm. 'Nobody knows', she said to herself. 'It could be years.' She looked out at the sky, aimlessly. An undefined, unknown time, like the length of our lives. We do not know when we will die, and we think, naively, that such a day will never come. Or still more naively, we feel it coming at any and every moment — this limitless, infinite tragedy that we shoulder like an eternal burden.

The tragedy would have been easier to bear had she been told that Saleem would be out in five, ten or even twenty years. Then she might have been able to cope. Waiting for a definite period of time is bearable, when we know when it will end and it can be precisely defined. But to live in the grip of parallel lines that never meet, to be trapped between two jaws never knowing when they will snap shut: this is our tragedy, the secret of the sadness that envelops our joys and the indifferent merriment that surrounds our grief. We know that we are fooling ourselves, that we are gripped by a will not our own, and that this other will must destroy us in the end, though we never know when.

Now, as the car raced along, Bahiah felt gripped by fate: one wrong movement of the car and she would be a crushed corpse. But when she looked at him she realized that she lay in the grip not of fate but of those big hands grasping the steering wheel. One false move by those hands would be enough to destroy both her and the car.

A strange feeling of indifference came over her. The car swerved suddenly and almost collided with another, but she was not afraid. True indifference comes when one realizes the futility of one's intentional life and untimed death, the futility of living indefinitely in chains. True indifference comes when one knows that death may come at any moment — why not this one rather than another?

She heard Dr Alawi's voice. 'I'd like to have lunch with you today. Is it all right?'

His politeness and hesitancy surprised her. Had he said, 'I'd like to throw you into the Nile. Is that all right?' she would have agreed straightaway, but he was only inviting her to lunch. That seemed insignificant compared with an invitation to die, so she said passively, 'All right.'

They drove along a shady tree-lined road. She knew only a few parts of Cairo and she felt she was now somewhere she had never been before, but she asked no questions. She silently enjoyed that comfortable feeling of indifference. She heard him say, 'Why have you left college?'

She answered sarcastically, 'They married me off.'

He laughed and took her hand. 'Are you kidding?'

'No', she said. 'No kidding. They married me off.'

His eyes widened in feigned astonishment. 'And what have you done about it?'

'I ran away', she said quietly.

He laughed again. 'You'll be dragged off to the House of Obedience.'

She laughed and turned her face to the sun. When he saw her black raised eyes, her upturned nose and her pursed lips, he asked, 'How are you going to live?'

She shook her short tousled hair and said, 'I'll work and manage somehow.'

'They'll look for you everywhere.'

'They'll never find me', she said confidently.

'It's not easy to hide in a city like Cairo. There are eyes everywhere. All the authorities are against you.'

She glanced cautiously at the street and looked at him searchingly.

'And you're against me too, aren't you?'

He smiled, 'I might have been against you, but I love you.'

The words sounded strange. She almost asked 'What does that mean?' but she pursed her lips in silence. The car stopped at a small house ringed by a garden. He took a key from his pocket and opened the door. She found herself in a large room with coloured wallpaper, pink curtains. A statue of a naked black woman stood over the fireplace, and on the wall hung a painting of another nude woman. She looked around in surprise and he smiled, saying, 'I slave all day at the college, the hospital and the clinic just for a few moments of happiness in this hide-out.'

He took off his jacket and the banknotes in the inside pocket smelt like the hospital — a mixture of blood and sweat and sick, panting breaths. She looked away and he handed her a glass, saying, 'This is an Egyptian wine called Omar Khayyam. The best wine in the world. What do you think?'

'I have no idea', she replied listlessly. 'I've never tasted wine before, Egyptian or foreign.'

He looked at her sad black eyes. 'I have a philosophy of life', he said. 'To live from day to day. I never think about yesterday or tomorrow. You should do the same, starting now.'

'I have a different philosophy', she said quietly.

He laughed out loud. 'A beautiful woman needs no philosophy.'

She did not laugh. He stretched out his hand, took hers and kissed it. 'Bahiah, I love you! Don't you know what love means?'

'No', she answered clearly.

His hands caressed her and he pressed her to his chest. She felt the quick beat of his heart. He held both her wrists in one hand and started to undress her with the other. She kicked at him strongly and he fell. As he picked himself up, he stared at her in astonishment. She was even more surprised than he was. He sat on a chair near the fireplace. 'It seems I've made a mistake', he said. 'I thought you were in love with me.'

'Where on earth did you get that idea?' she answered in amazement.

'I understand women', he said in his lecturer's tone.

'With what brain?'

He pointed to his head and smiled. 'Man has only one brain, in his head. Didn't I teach you that in the dissecting room?'

'The dissecting room is one thing, the truth is another', she replied scornfully.

'What is the truth?'

'That a man's brain is not in his head.'

'Where then?'

'Between his legs', she answered boldly.

He put on his jacket, saying, 'You're not normal, girl.'

'You're a perfectly normal man', she said smiling.

She strode out proudly. 'Not normal.' And what do they consider a normal girl? One with beaten eyes who walks with closely-bound legs, obedient and submissive, with amputated sexual organs? One who drips with perfumed powders and paints, saturated day and night with sad songs and sex films? One who knows romantic stories by heart and can't really experience anything? The virtuous and pure virgin preoccupied with removing body hair and enticing men?

She walked along with her quick, long strides, looking left and right, inspecting people's faces. The street was full of them. Their faces, their movements, their voices were all similar. When she looked at their eyes she did not see them. She felt she was drowning with no one to see or recognize her and that her face was becoming like that of Aliah, Zakiah, Najiah or Yvonne.

Absent-mindedly, she ran in the direction of al-Muqattam street. Her eyes searched earth, trees and sky for those eyes that were capable of seeing her, for the thin face with the intense features burdened by people's cares. 'Saleem!' she shouted. But the mountain swallowed her voice and its echo. 'Saleem!' she cried out still louder. No one answered, but she did not turn back.

She knew he was there, like the sky, the air, the sun, the moon and the stars. He was part of the universe. She breathed him every minute, she felt his touch on her body as she walked, sat or slept. When she gazed at the sky she saw his eyes in its blueness. She saw his nose in every high, pointed arch. With each step she took she heard his footsteps. She almost turned to see him but stopped herself. She knew he was not there, that the sky was empty of him, that the earth was devoid of people, and that the universe was hollow like an empty box whose air has been sucked out by a magic pump.

'Bahiah!' His voice rang out behind her and she started, but no one was there. She pulled herself together. In that determined gesture, she realized that she would go to him, she would devote her life to going to him, and nothing could stand between them, not death, bullets, blood, the sharp lancet cutting into flesh, the high iron door, the lock.

She took long, fast strides as if she knew where she was going, but soon she stopped. She did not know where to go. When she looked around she saw her father's head through the window of a taxi. Beside him was her uncle and someone else, a strange head that she seemed to glimpse through thick fog. Suddenly she remembered her wedding night. Panting, she hid behind a wall. The taxi drove on and was swallowed up by the traffic. She came out and walked on with her straight, strong legs. She knew the sound of her footsteps, one after the other, as she stamped the ground in defiance. She would lift one foot high and bring it down hard as if penetrating the earth and defying the whole world around her. She would kick anyone who approached her and gouge out the eyes of anyone who dared to touch her or even to stir the air

113

around her. With her lancet she would rip open the belly of anyone who stood in her way. Yes, she would kill him. She was capable of committing murder. In fact, nothing but the crime of murder could extinguish the fire now burning within her.

It was three o'clock in the morning, just before dawn. Darkness ruled the narrow mud streets. The old houses leaned against each other for support like the skeletons of sick bodies. The breaths of the Dirassah neighbourhood, with its small overcrowded rooms, steamed out through the windows, carrying the dust of the mountain and the smell of sweat, onion, lentils and rice, and fried fish. This area, a hive of activity in the daytime, was now fast asleep, the sleep of exhausted bodies so similar to death. Now and then a dog barked, a baby cried, or a cat miaowed, breaking the silence.

But life was in full swing in the basement of the old house. The small printing press covered the white paper with black characters. When one sheet was fully printed the machine would spin and a fresh sheet would be sucked in, soon to be filled with black lines and replaced in turn by a new sheet of paper. The three thin faces were pale and exhausted. Six staring eyes followed the circular movement of the paper. One pair of dark eyes looked up in a familiar way. They were intensely black. The nose was sharp and upturned, dividing the world in two. The lips were pursed in determination and anger.

'Bahiah!' The voice rang in her ear. She looked around to see Raouf stuffing the papers into the leather bag, and Fawzi hiding the printing press in a hole in the floor and replacing the floorboards. The small wooden door creaked in the silence and the three people slipped out, one after the other. No one would have recognized her: their features looked alike in the dark. Her legs were sinewy inside her trousers and a bulging leather bag dangled from her right hand.

In the small square Raouf turned right and was swallowed up by the dark street. Fawzi headed for the main square. Bahiah strode towards the waiting bus, her chest heaving, her breath coming in gasps. She clutched the bulging leather bag to her chest, cradling it like a mother cuddling her baby. She would get off at the next stop. She knew where to go. She knew where to take the blazing words.

'People of Egypt! Awake! Throw open your windows, open your eyes and see the chains coiled around your necks! Open your minds and see that the sweat of your brows is being plundered. Your crops are stolen, your flesh devoured until you are left only skin and bones, queueing skeletons each leaning on the other. Your breath is torn by fits of coughing and blood pours from a deep wound in your chest.'

She hurled the words and letters at the faces and returned with the empty bag, free from her burden, hopping like a sparrow and humming an old tune. She swung the empty bag like a child returning happily from school. She tossed it in the air and caught it as it fell. She saw the man with the spying eyes walking cautiously after her. She glanced at him out of the corner of her eye. When she decided that he was following her she turned into another road, slipped away from him and returned to the main street, to be swallowed up by the sea of people. She walked along, observing people on the treadmill of their daily lives. The tram with its uneven steps creaked under the weight of bodies. Its iron wheels hungered for any stumbling foot. On the platform an old, blind woman sat stretching out her veined hand. Children looked out at the world with yellow eyes, their gaping mouths hungry for any bite that came their way. In the windows of the tram and the bus she could see the identical heads and necks hanged by their ties. She saw the bulging, frightened eyes and heard the murmured incantations. Occasionally a black car like a police car sped by. Through shining windows she saw fleshy faces with their narrow, spying eyes.

At nightfall she strode back towards her small attic room. Her panting breath came like a stifled sob. Streaks of sweat ran down her face and armpits. She pulled the iron bar down across the door, clamped all the windows shut and stretched out on the small iron bed, gazing into the darkness. The thin, intense face, the blue-black eyes able to see her loomed before her. 'Saleem!' she called out faintly, but no one answered. Realizing that she was alone, she got up, pulled the painting out from under the bed and stood it against the wall. The pressure of her hand as it coiled around the brush gave her a mysterious joy that spread from her fingers to her arms, neck and head as if along a taut electric wire.

Anyone seeing her there in the dark would have been astonished. Her muscles were as taut as if she had been crucified. Her black eyes were fixed on her lines, her head steady, her arm confident. Her fingers gripped the brush and her feet were solid like a granite statue.

117

No one could know how long she would stay like that. The whole night might pass as she sat, immobile, adding no lines to her painting: but her eyes never shifted. She relived her life, saw it parade before her eyes, moment by moment, like a film.

Shortly before dawn she moved her brush over the painting, changing the lines and creating new moments in her life, new moments that she chose to create through her own will. With that deliberate movement across the paper — in any and all directions — she destroyed other wills and designed her own lines and features. She would make her eyes blacker, her nose more upturned and her lips pursed in ever greater anger and determination.

When she felt tired she would let her body fall and stretch out on the iron bed. She shivered under the old blanket, pulling it over her head and around her freezing feet. Her teeth chattered, making a faint sound like a baby sparrow that had fallen from its mother's nest in an arid land, trembling as its tearful eyes glowed in the dark with the frightened look of an orphan.

A hot tear ran from the corner of her eye onto the pillow. She felt its wet warmth on her cheek and peeped out from under the blanket to see her mother: the long thin face like her own, the wide black eyes, and the breast that offered generous warmth. She buried her head in her mother's breast, sniffing her and seeking an opening that would contain her, hoping to hide from the world and the forces threatening her. She wanted to curl up like a foetus. Her body shook with a strange violent yearning for security. She longed to curl up in her mother's womb, to feel security, silence, with no sound or movement. Her mother's big arms embraced her with amazing strength, pulling her body towards her once more.

With all her might she tried to make their bodies one, but in vain. The eternal separation took place in a fleeting moment never to return.

'Bahiah!' The voice rang out and she opened her eyes. But no one was there. The sun had started to penetrate the rotting wood of the shutters. She heard the slow knocks from behind the door that greeted her every day. She saw the old man with his turban, kaftan, grey eyes in which the white seemed to have melted into the iris, his thick brown fingers curled round the yellow worry beads, moving them fast and regularly like a constant shiver. The same shiver could be seen in his thin yellow lips, which muttered incomprehensible words in which the letter s recurred like a whistle.

When he saw her, the gap between his dry lips widened and the edges of his decaying yellow teeth appeared. He whispered in a voice like a sleeping snake, 'Are you awake?'

'No', she answered angrily, and closed the door. She heard him hiss behind the door. He was an old man whose lungs had been destroyed by smoking. He had bled his life away in the beds of four frigid, virtuous wives: each had given birth to a number of children, half of whom were dead, the others married off. He had only one wife left, an old woman who propped herself against the wall, made him black tea and set up the water pipe for him in the evening. He would lie near her in the wooden bed and bury his thick fingers between her sagging breasts. Their thin bodies would shake wearily and their cold stagnant breath would be visited by a faint glimmer of warmth, soon to disappear like a death rattle, leaving them like two corpses in their old wooden bed.

She wrapped up the painting and went out the small

wooden door, her tall body slim, her straight legs enveloped by her trousers. One foot trod firmly on the ground before the other, and her legs parted noticeably. The men of the neighbourhood gazed at her from the shops; the women stared through keyholes and cracks in the windows. Was she woman or man? Had it not been for the two small breasts showing through the blouse, they would have sworn she was a man. But since she was a woman, it was legitimate to stare. Her body was the victim of hungry, deprived eyes. They stared at her and whispered. One dared to laugh obscenely, another made a dirty crack. Street urchins were encouraged to follow her, wiggling their bottoms. Teenage boys would expose themselves to her. One threw a stone, another let out a long cat-call. Men sitting in the cafe laughed hoarsely, slapping their thighs with rough hands cracked like arid, thirsty land. Women would strike their breasts and heave that ever-suppressed feminine sigh, saying, 'Just look at what Western women are like!'

She fought her way through stares, noise and obscene remarks. She raised her black eyes and pursed her lips in anger, defying fate. Once she disappeared down the street, life in the neighbourhood returned to normal. The blacksmith's hammer and anvil rang out; the clinking of glasses and the click-clack of backgammon could be heard in the cafe; children crying, boys fighting and women quarrelling were heard from behind the cracks — and also the coarse voices of men taking the oath to divorce their wives. The smell of boiled fish, *falafel*, rice and lentils was everywhere. Worry beads danced in the hands of the old man sitting on his prayer mat by the window. When he bowed down, his body touched the wool of the carpet: he would be overcome by suppressed

desire, and his old eyes would search the neighbourhood for any plump body.

When she reached the main street she felt a wave of
cold air hit her burning cheeks. The muscles of her
face contracted and a sense of impending danger
swept through her body. From the corner of her eye
she glimpsed the policeman standing there, then she
went into a small shop and unwrapped her painting.
The old man smiled, as he usually did on seeing her
work. His veined hand reached into his pocket and
extracted three Egyptian pounds, which he counted
out carefully, one after the other.

She went back out into the street, and soon realized
that a pair of eyes were watching her and footsteps
following her. A bakery smell reached her nose; she
went in and ate a piece of her favourite cake. When she
paid the cashier, she saw the narrow eyes behind her
in the mirror. She went out into the street and hailed a
taxi, glancing at her watch. The taxi stopped. At a
bend in the street she looked behind her and saw the
same pair of eyes following in another taxi. She got out
at al-Attabah square. She knew that Raouf and Fawzi
would be waiting for her in the basement but she did
not join them. She wandered down al-Moski street,
watching the women and girls as they walked with
their closely-bound fat legs, pounding the street with
their bodies, their bottoms visible under their glossy
dresses. Their made-up eyes devoured the shop
windows: they lusted after clothes, transparent nightdresses, slippers, make-up, perfume and body
lotions. Their sharp, penetrating voices mingled with
the popping of chewing gum and the clacking of
pointed high heels bearing bodies laden with shop-
ping.

She pursed her lips in anger, for the greedy desire to

consume is mere compensation for eternal depriva-tion. Under the lustful, burning eyes lies the coldness of snow. Under the hair wavy as silk lies a brain soft like a rabbit's, knowing nothing of life except eating and reproduction.

The sun was setting as she went out into the street. The sky, the earth, the houses and trees were tinged pale red. They grew paler by the minute, like a face drained of blood after the long, slow wait for death. Then the street lights came on. Hundreds of white circles of light were reflected on the asphalt, in shop windows, in car windscreens and in people's faces. Everything glowed under the light. She heard soft laughter and saw a girl taking a young man's arm while his other arm curled around her. She smiled at them as a sudden energy surged through her. She filled her lungs with the damp night air. Her black eyes glittered like diamonds as, with childish joy, she watched the coloured lights hanging like balloons from the stores. She watched the cars speeding over the shiny asphalt, the window-panes glistening like mirrors, and the people in their colourful clothes walking in the white light like herds of deer. A child let off a firework: the rocket exploded in millions of shining, coloured particles.

She heard herself laugh as she had as a child. She almost skipped like a child too, but then she saw the narrow eyes in front of her. She turned and saw another pair of eyes watching her. She went down a side street on her right but found that the eyes blocked her way. She headed for her own neighbourhood, but the policeman's fat body loomed with his shiny buttons and his pointed weapon hanging from his leather belt.

She stopped and looked around quickly with that

frantic movement of people who feel threatened, with known and unknown forces lying in wait to destroy them. The eyes dart in all directions, watching for the hand that may strike from front or back, left or right. The head jerks continuously: every cell is alert, thinking: how can I save myself from the impending danger? How can I protect my body from the blows and carry it away safely? The muscles contract cautiously; the heart beats impatiently; the blood surges through the body with its rapid, regular pulse: it is the throb of anxiety, bringing with it the sensation of life. Her long, fine fingers shook imperceptibly. Her feet stood firm, the outlines of her body as unyielding as the earth beneath her feet. But under that stillness was a rapid, palpable movement, like the vibrations of air sensed by the ear or the pulse of blood through the walls of the veins. It was a rapid vibration that seemed silent from the outside — but beneath the stillness was hidden a frightening violent motion. It was the struggle between resistance and submission, the only movement through which the difference between life and death becomes clear.

It was a frightening moment. She feared it as much as she desired it. She longed to escape from it and yearned to pursue it. It was the only time she saw that she was real and alive. We feel alive only when we face death. It is like the colour white that becomes white only when contrasted with black.

Her lips parted in a smile and her eyes shone. This moment was her goal. She had wanted it from the very beginning and had marched toward it firmly and with determination. She knew that she was heading only toward danger, and at its brink was that small place, just a foot wide suspended in air; above was sky and below the abyss. It was a moment ruled by two powerful forces: one pulling down to the abyss, the other urging soaring flight.

She was sure that she would not plunge into the abyss. She would not surrender. She would not be Bahiah Shaheen, would not return to the ordinary faces, would not sink into the sea of similar bodies or tumble into the grave of ordinary life.

She raised her black eyes, tensed the muscles of her back and legs and walked toward them with long strides, each foot striking sharply on the ground, her legs parting confidently and freely. When she was face to face with them she said in her quiet, confident voice, 'Let's go!'

One of them locked the handcuffs around her wrists and put the key in his pocket. She walked briskly in front of them, her eyes darting, her feet searching among all those faces for the thin face with the exhausted features burdened with the world's worries, for those eyes that could pick out her face from all other faces and distinguish her body from among millions of bodies floating in the universe.

When she saw him before her she shouted joyfully like a child: 'Saleem!'

She stretched out her arms to embrace him, but she could not reach, and her hands trembled in the handcuffs.

Nawal el–Saadawi has gained a considerable reputation in the English–speaking world through her books *The Hidden Face of Eve,* a study of women in Arab society, and *Woman at Point Zero,* a novel. She lives in Cairo, where she works as a doctor.